NURSE OF THE CROSSROADS

COLLEEN L. REECE

THORNDIKE
CHIVERS

This Large Print edition is published by Thorndike Press, Waterville, Maine, USA and by BBC Audiobooks Ltd, Bath, England.
Thorndike Press, a part of Gale, Cengage Learning.
Copyright © 1977 by Colleen L. Reece.
The moral right of the author has been asserted.

LIBRARY OF CONGRESS CATALOGING-IN-PUBLICATION DATA

Reece, Colleen L.
  Nurse of the Crossroads / by Colleen L. Reece.
    p. cm. — (Thorndike Press large print candlelight)
  ISBN-13: 978-1-4104-0459-6 (hardcover : alk. paper)
  ISBN-10: 1-4104-0459-5 (hardcover : alk. paper)
  1. Nurses — Fiction. 2. Large type books. I. Title.
PS3568.E3646N89 2008
813'.54—dc22   2007044618

BRITISH LIBRARY CATALOGUING-IN-PUBLICATION DATA AVAILABLE
Published in 2008 in the U.S. by arrangement with Colleen L. Reece.
Published in 2008 in the U.K. by arrangement with the author.
U.K. Hardcover: 978 1 405 64410 5 (Chivers Large Print)
U.K. Softcover: 978 1 405 64411 2 (Camden Large Print)

Printed in the United States of America
1 2 3 4 5 6 7 11 10 09 08

Nurse of the Crossroads

CHAPTER 1

The lone figure etched against the threatening sky pulled his coat closer against the rising wind. Shivering in the cold, he called himself a fool for being there. No one in his right mind, not even an ace reporter, could find a story in a simple country graveyard — or could he? He looked again at the small stone marking a new grave, reading its inscription for the third time:

DAVID MACKENZIE
who accepted the
Crossroads Calling

What enigmatic words to mark the passing of a life! Reluctantly, he turned away and got in his car, still looking around the unfamiliar country. Rolling hills, now lightly touched with a frosting of snow gave way to higher, tree-covered mountains. They in turn melted into the distant snow-covered peaks barely visible in the growing dusk. There was a wild beauty here, the reporter admitted to himself, but there was something else, something unexplainable. Determinedly he started the motor. He wouldn't take the assignment, that was all there was to it! He would tell the chief to get someone else. And yet — he remembered the look in his Chief Editor's eyes as he called Sam to his office the day before.

"Sam, there's a story I want you to cover. Read this."

Sam obediently glanced over the obituary. It was nothing special. Curious, he returned it to the chief.

"I didn't expect you to recognize the name, Sam. David Mackenzie dropped out of sight many years ago. Few will remember him now, but at one time he was the Chief of Staff of Memorial Hospital here in Portland. He was also my personal friend."

The chief hesitated for a moment, then continued. "It sounds strange I suppose coming from me, but that man was more than a doctor! He believed he was a partner of God, and that his skill was beyond himself." He looked embarrassed for a moment, then glanced up in time to see the cynical smile on Sam's face.

"Laugh if you want to. David Mackenzie

had something few men ever possess. He talked with God the way you and I talk."

In spite of his amusement Sam felt a faint spark of interest. This David Mackenzie really must have had something to impress a hard nut like Don Baker! Almost eagerly he bent forward. "And then?"

The chief gazed unseeing out the window. "That's the mystery, Sam. There wasn't any 'and then . . .' "

Sam was all ears now, his keen sense of reporting ready for a story.

"Mystery? Why a mystery?"

"At the height of a brilliant medical career, David Mackenzie submitted his resignation. He gave no reason whatsoever. Without warning and over the protest of the entire hospital he left the work he loved and the fame he had achieved. He walked away from honors, fortune, a beautiful home." Don Baker paused, an angry look crossing his face.

"Can you believe any man would willingly give up what he did for apparently non-existent reasons? In spite of speculation, the usual talk, no one has ever discovered the real reason behind his resignation."

"But what happened to him?" Sam wanted to know. "And why this sudden interest in him now that he's dead?"

The editor's level gaze met Sam's squarely.

"David Mackenzie disappeared." At Sam's start of surprise, he nodded his shaggy gray head. "Yes, disappeared completely for over fifteen years. I made a few attempts to find him, but you know with the pressures of the *Star* I don't have much time either. Yet all these years there has been a gap in me, an emptiness that began soon after David went away." He looked sheepishly at Sam.

"The thing I missed most was the understanding between us, and when I pinpointed my feelings, I realized I was envious of David. Of all the men I ever knew, he was the one who stood without wavering for what he believed. He had something to believe in, which is more than most of us have. Over the years it has become an obsession with me. I've got to know whether David's beliefs were real! At one time I was almost ready to seek out whatever it was that made David Mackenzie the man he was. The God he believed in may not even exist, but for David He existed. I want to know everything there is to know about David Mackenzie from the time of his resignation until his death."

Sam was stunned. He had never guessed the depths of his chief. The tormented man in front of him was to the staff of the

Portland Star an inexorable but fair editor. But today . . .

"If you feel this way, why did you wait so long? Couldn't you have searched until you did find David Mackenzie, or if not him, ask some minister about all this?" Sam felt a stirring within himself even as he spoke.

"I couldn't," the chief replied, meeting Sam's level gaze. "I've never admitted it to another living soul, but I was afraid what I might find out. About five years ago I traced David to a tiny town in eastern Oregon. His mailing address was a rural route out of LaGrande. There's a crossroads there, and I found out David had started a tiny clinic. He was practically giving away his services. Many of the people who needed help were given medical aid without charge. People from miles around came to him."

"And you didn't contact him? Why?" There was scorn in Sam's voice.

"I told you. I couldn't. I had gone over the circumstances in my mind a hundred times, two hundred. At last I came up with what I felt had to be the answer. David Mackenzie must have known some scandal was going to break that would oust him from Portland Memorial. He must have gotten out before it could hit. There seems to be no other explanation. Either that, or he found out his faith in his God was a fairytale. I just didn't want to face whatever the reason was. Either way it would be the falling of an idol. I worshipped David Mackenzie and would have staked my life on his integrity. Yet was he a hypocrite? If I found out those things, I don't know what it would do to me. So I let it rest. Then today I saw this in the paper —" He motioned to the clipping. "I realized I had accused, tried, and convicted David in my mind. What kind of friend was I? It's been eating on me and now I've got to know! Don't you see, Sam, I've got to know!"

A bright spot of color touched Don Baker's cheeks and his voice was hoarse. He went on. "Right now I stand where David Mackenzie once stood. I have wealth, a certain amount of fame and prestige. Yet, unlike him, I don't have anything to believe in. I'm getting old. The years ahead will bring retirement, the usual round of golf, travel, and so on. But what then? There's a drive inside of me that tells me I must know what it was that kept David Mackenzie going. If it was false, my one remaining shred of hope is gone. You asked why I hadn't asked ministers about this. I have, many of them. But the ones I've encountered seem to know all about God — David Mackenzie knew God personally. If I ever believe in God, and perhaps I won't, I will have to become His partner, like David did. That's why, Sam, that's why I have to know. If there is nothing to it, if the finest man I have ever known found it all a dream, then I will go ahead living the way I do. But if he really had something . . ." His voice trailed off.

Sam's thoughts returned to the present. His car was warm now; it was time to go on into LaGrande. The visit to the graveyard had been fruitless, except for those cryptic words on the headstone, and yet —

"I can't give up!" he spoke aloud. "I'm just as hooked on finding out about this David Mackenzie as the chief is." His thoughts raced on. He remembered his chief's words:

"I'm sending you because you aren't easily swayed. If I go myself, I will go wanting to hear only the good, ready to excuse or overlook those things that might discredit David. You can be more objective, Sam. You can find out the story of the Crossroads Clinic." His grip was firm as they shook hands, but there was a look in his eyes that told Sam how much this assignment meant.

"I'll do my best," he promised.

"Take as much time as you need, and do it in any way you like," his editor told him. "But stay until you have the whole story."

Sam hadn't wasted any time. He had packed, taken his car in for servicing, and told his landlady he would be away for a time. She was used to his comings and goings and only smiled, promising to forward his mail to General Delivery, LaGrande.

The trip up the Columbia Gorge had been breathtaking. It was autumn, the colors were beautiful. Sam had driven the Gorge many times, but somehow this time it was different. Was it because a thrill of anticipation filled him? His senses were keen. Everywhere he looked was beauty. Dark green firs and pines bordered the hills on the south of the highway; the mighty Columbia River was on the north. An unusual amount of water poured over the high cliff of Multnomah Falls to cascade into the shimmering pool at the bottom. Everywhere he looked the red and gold of fall was dotting the green background. As he got closer to LaGrande, he could see frosted mountaintops. He was glad he had thrown in his snow tires and chains. If this assignment took a long time, he would be prepared. He had noticed that glorious Mt. Hood was snow-capped, shining in the sunlight, and had stopped to take pictures. At least he could get some other stories if David Mackenzie's proved to be worthless.

A pang went through him at the thought. Was he on the brink of something he could only guess at now? Why should he care what he found, except that he knew his editor would be deeply hurt if his friend turned out to be a disappointment? Then too, it had all happened so long ago. Maybe no one in this small town would even care about Dr. Mackenzie's past. He might not get the story after all.

Sam's jaw set. If there was a story, he would get it.

By the time he reached the motel he had chosen, lazy flakes were drifting down. He had liked the looks of the individual pine log cabins the motel offered, the geraniums in the window boxes, the welcome of the owners. He had planned to try various places for a night, choosing the most convenient for his home base, but after examining the complete cabin, with its tiny fireplace, inviting chair where he could write, he signed for a week.

Sam decided it was too cold to bother with a restaurant that night. There was a tiny kitchenette in his cabin, and plenty of sandwiches left from the lunch his landlady had packed. He would make coffee and stay in.

It certainly was going to be a cosy place

to work. A sigh of pure enjoyment went through him as he dropped into the chair by the fireplace after touching off the well-laid fire. The kindling caught immediately, and the dancing flames reflected his thoughts as he stared at them unseeingly. Tomorrow he would lay in a supply of canned goods. If he didn't want to go out he could easily keep himself well fed. He would have all the comforts of home.

He smiled wryly to himself. Home! The word was a travesty in his life. Raised in a poor family, clawing his way out of the slums, he hadn't had much time for a home. He also hadn't had much time to seek out anything such as this David Mackenzie had. Sam wasn't an atheist, although those at the *Star* considered him one; he just hadn't found anything really big to believe in. The Christianity he had seen was the one-day-a-week kind, and he had no use for hypocrisy.

A strange stirring, a longing for something he had never known filled Sam now as he sat in the warm cabin with snowflakes dancing on his window. The feeling was mingled with sadness. If he did find out that David Mackenzie's life was tainted, what then? How would it affect his chief? How would it affect himself? Rudely he pushed the thought aside. What difference would there be? He didn't believe in anything now, did he, so how could a dead man affect him? Yet deep inside he realized he had become more involved with this story than any other he had ever done. Something about Don Baker had triggered off his own emotional responses, he reasoned, knowing full well it was more than that.

Throughout the evening before the fire Sam would resolutely crowd the thoughts back, only to have them overwhelm him. To get away from his own feelings he took out a large map of the surrounding area and pored over it.

"Go to the smaller towns around LaGrande," his chief had advised. "It is my understanding that often Dr. Mackenzie would go into Wallowa, Enterprise, Minam Canyon, even to the lodge at Wallowa Lake. He worked with other local doctors, and they knew him well. Go see them. Find out who and what he became. Besides" — he grinned — "you need a vacation and those mountains provide some of the most beautiful scenery on the West Coast. Take some time off to roam through the forests, or just sit and look at those hills and mountains."

He paused, then continued. "I wish I could go with you. You know, Sam" — there was an unaccustomed tenderness in the old man's voice — "since my wife died, it has been pretty lonesome. We never had children and when you came to work with us it was kind of like the boy I wanted. We've worked together on the paper, the way I would have wanted my son to do. Someday, if you are interested, maybe you could take over the editorship. It would be almost as though I had had a son to follow in my footsteps." Not giving Sam a chance to reply, he resumed his gruff manner.

"Now get out there and get me my story!"

Sam's eyes were moist with unaccustomed feeling as he remembered his chief's words. He had learned to respect the crusty editor, and since the day before, had seen an entirely different person. The staff little suspected what lay beyond the extremely efficient chief of the *Star.*

The fire had gone out, leaving little white trails of smoke, and the cabin was getting cold as Sam prepared for bed. When the lights were out his last waking thought was, Tomorrow I'll go out to that Crossroads Clinic. Strange. I've never heard of an inscription like the one they used for him, "David Mackenzie — who accepted the Crossroads Calling." Wonder what it means? Well, anyway, it will be a place to start.

Outside the cabin the snow ceased, replaced with crisp coldness. One by one the stars peeked through the cloud cover until at last they joined the moon in looking down on the new world Sam had entered. Little had he realized as he punched down his pillow just what this assignment would mean in the life of his chief — and in his own. There was no way at this point he could have known the truth about David Mackenzie, yet this assignment would bring Sam a story more meaningful than headlines, more to be treasured than gold. He was only beginning to sense that some power was calling, no, not calling, but compelling him to drop everything else in his life and learn the story of the strange inscription he had read.

CHAPTER 2

A few miles out of LaGrande a dimly lit sign outside a small building proclaimed to a disinterested world that this was the Crossroads Clinic. The building was as unassuming as the sign, a little worn, a little rundown. A somewhat newer attachment gave the impression that living quarters had been built on as an afterthought, and from the window framed in early American curtains a brighter light shone, making a patch in the front yard.

Shivering in the cold, Amber Mackenzie hurriedly turned up the heat and threw another chunk into the fireplace. Her hands were numb from the drive down Minam Canyon. Her white uniform and cap were crumpled, and there were shadows of weariness beneath the beautiful eyes. Her short golden-brown hair was the exact color of those eyes, and Amber was a fitting name for such a golden girl. At last she was thawed enough to remove her jacket and hang it in the tiny closet, pull the curtains against the cold outdoors, and sink into a chair, too tired and discouraged to move.

I should eat, she thought dully as she sat, gradually letting the peace of the homey but shabby room sink into her very being. At last she roused enough to heat some soup and make toast, but once back by the fire she looked at it in distaste and pushed it aside.

"What am I going to do?" she whispered to herself. Her mind flashed back to the evening just past. She had accompanied Dr. Robert Meacham up the canyon to where a group of hikers had packed out. One of them had had the misfortune to break an ankle. The ambulance was ready and waiting when the group got to the paved road, and there had been little time for personalities, yet she had felt Dr. Meacham's eyes on her as she deftly handed him the necessary equipment to temporarily ease the man's suffering.

They had taken him on into LaGrande, and it was Amber who had scrubbed and assisted in the necessary followup treatment. The man had a bad break, and by the time they had finished Amber was exhausted.

Dr. Meacham apologized. "I'm sorry, Amber. I know it's been hard on you with just losing your father, but we really do need you. We're shorthanded from the flu epidemic." He had insisted on driving her home, and on the way had brought up the question that had haunted her ever since her father died. "What are your plans?"

She could only shrug mutely. She really didn't know.

"I've already had an offer for the clinic," she told him. "A semi-retired doctor came the day of the funeral. He wants to buy it and use it as the nucleus of a nursing home. He says that although it is small it is well equipped, and he has the money to back building several small cottage-type accommodations surrounding it. He is very enthusiastic about it." She stopped abruptly.

"But what about you?" Dr. Meacham insisted gently.

"I don't know. He asked me to stay on, but they would need my present quarters. Besides, I don't know if I would want to use my nursing ability just in a nursing home. I've always liked working with all ages. That's one reason I insisted on coming back to the Crossroads Clinic after I finished training. Dad wouldn't have urged me, but I really loved it. I felt part of a team, helping him care for some of those who wouldn't have sought it elsewhere."

She smiled wanly. "Besides, I'll miss my 'outdoor public health nursing.' "

Dr. Meacham laughed outright. It was a standing battle between them. In the year Amber had been home, she had often taken routine calls to some of the outlying areas in the surrounding mountains. Dr. Meacham firmly believed that if there was something wrong with a person, he belonged in a hospital. Dr. Mackenzie and Amber felt that if it was something that could be cared for at home, many times that was the better way to go. Yet there was warm affection between them. Amber had known Robert since they were much younger. She had tagged after him, a serious little five-year-old following his lead. Even then, at twelve years of age, he had known he would be a doctor. It had been he rather than her own father who persuaded her to enter nurse's training. She would have been content to stay home and keep house for her father. But now she was glad she had earned her R.N. It would serve her in good stead no matter what she decided to do.

"There's always a place for you in my office," Robert told her quietly, a tender note in his voice. Amber shied away from committing herself. She knew Robert had loved her for years, but although she thought of him as a dear brother, the feelings she had were not strong enough for marriage — at least not yet. If she went into his office, the very closeness in their working arrangement would force a decision she didn't want to make. Sometimes she felt she should marry Robert simply because he was so good, yet in her heart she knew that if she did, it would be cheating him as well as herself. He was willing to wait, confident that in time Amber would turn to him.

Sighing wearily, she rose and prepared for bed. Maybe she should go away for a while. But where? She loved this place dearly. Her father had seen to it that she went on trips, often taking her himself after her mother had died. Still, no place she had seen could compare in Amber's eyes. Too tired to think of it longer, she snapped out the light and crawled into bed, but not to sleep. Her mind raced, considering and rejecting possibilities. It was hours before she slept, and when she did, it was only to be haunted by fragments of dreams, troubled, without solution.

She was awakened by the sound of the telephone. It was still early, not yet eight o'clock. The clinic never opened until nine.

24

Who could be calling at this time of day?

A masculine voice spoke. "Is this the Crossroads Clinic? The one where Dr. Mackenzie worked?"

Shaken by some odd note in the unfamiliar voice, Amber replied, "This is Amber Mackenzie. May I help you?"

There was a moment's silence on the other end of the line, then a rather disconcerted voice asked, "You are Dr. Mackenzie's daughter?"

"Yes, I am," Amber said crisply. "Who is calling, please?"

"Miss Mackenzie, this is Sam Reynolds, of the *Portland Star.* You don't know me, but I work for an old friend of your father, Don Baker of the *Star.* He asked me to come to LaGrande. May I see you?"

Amber hesitated. In spite of his words she felt a bit uneasy.

"Did Mr. Baker tell you to see me?"

"No, I am quite sure he is unaware of your existence. Wait," he pleaded as she began to speak. "If you would only have a few minutes free today I could explain in person much better than trying to tell you over the telephone." He added as an afterthought, "I will bring my credentials, of course, so you can see I really work for the *Star.*"

"All right," the girl agreed reluctantly.

"But it will have to be later today. Could you come after four? The clinic closes then."

"Yes, I could," he replied, "but I thought your father . . ."

"I keep the clinic open for routine treatments," she told him.

"I'll be there at four," he promised.

True to his word, Sam stood in the clinic doorway promptly at four o'clock. The room was empty for the moment, but in a few minutes a stout woman came from an inner room with a smiling girl ushering her out.

"Now take care of that arm," she told the woman. "I'll re-dress the burn tomorrow at the same time." Glancing curiously at the stranger, the woman went out, and Amber turned to Sam. The sunlight streamed through the still-open door, flooding her with light. In her white uniform and cap she looked like a golden goddess.

Sam rubbed his eyes, his heart beating wildly. Was it possible to fall in love at first sight? She was beautiful. In his confusion he failed to notice the clear red blush his stare had brought to her face.

"Well?" she asked directly.

Sam fumbled in his pocket and silently laid his press card on the desk. She picked it up, read it slowly, then handed it back to him. There was a slight frown on her lovely face.

"I don't know what you would want to see me for," she told him.

Recovering his poise, Sam said, "I want to know about your father."

"My father?" She stared in surprise. "Why would a Portland reporter want to know about my father? He's dead now." Her fingers trembled as she laced them together, and one tear slipped down her cheek.

Suddenly Sam felt uncomfortable. It was easy enough to assure his chief he would get to the bottom of the story of David Mackenzie. It was something else to face this beautiful daughter and demand the truth. He decided to use strategy. After all, the chief had told him to get the story in his own way. Now was the time to start.

"Don Baker loved your father as he loved perhaps no other friend," he told Amber. "All these years while they have been out of touch he has wondered about him. Now he feels he must know about him." Meeting Amber's eyes he added quickly, "Would you tell me about the Crossroads Clinic?"

"That is rather a large order," she told him seriously. She hesitated, then asked, "Would you like to come back to my quarters? It is much more comfortable."

Curiously he followed the beautiful girl into the shabby room. She entered as though it were a palace and seated herself near the fireplace, motioning him to a chair across from her. For a moment he didn't know where to begin. Seeing his confusion, Amber took pity on him. She didn't know exactly what this stocky, sandy-haired giant of a man wanted to know, but he was certainly having a hard time asking! A wicked gleam came into her eyes.

"How did you hear about the Crossroads Clinic?"

Sam found himself telling her how his editor had called him in and asked him to go to LaGrande. He omitted the real reason. Amber's keen gaze seemed to see straight through him.

"I see. The editor of a large city paper was interested enough in a small wayside clinic to send a reporter clear across a state to get a story on it?"

The lightly veiled sarcasm in her voice stung Sam more than he cared to admit. He wasn't doing so well.

Suddenly dropping his pose, he decided to tell her the truth.

"Miss Mackenzie, my editor is a hard man, a businessman. Yet there was something about your father that drew him. He saw in David Mackenzie a peace, some kind of inner faith that most men search for and fail to find." He was unaware of the wistful note that crept into his voice, but Amber caught it and something within her responded.

"When your father left his position as Chief of Staff of Portland Memorial so many years ago, the city was in an uproar. No one knew why. Then many years passed and he turned up here, in this tiny village, with a small clinic. Why? This is what Don Baker wants to know. Why? How could he leave his home, his friends, his fortune? You were only a child when it happened. Do you remember much about it?"

Amber gazed at him wide-eyed. This was no nosy reporter, this was a man with a quest. She sensed the answers he sought were vitally important not only to his editor but to himself. A spark lit her eyes. What an opportunity to show her father as he had really been! This was her chance to tell the world the real story behind the Crossroads Clinic.

Abruptly she spoke. "I will tell you everything you wish to know. It is a strange story. You may not believe parts of it. At times I think it was hard even for my father to accept all of what happened. Yet it is true. I will only ask one thing of you. After you have heard the story, you may want to print it, or parts of it. If you do, I must have your promise that no matter what you personally feel about it, the story must not be told in ridicule, or in sarcasm. If you cannot write it as it happened, then it must remain untold. My father's memory shall never be scorned by those who cannot accept anything except what they see."

Something in her level gaze brought Sam's hand out as he promised, "It will be as you wish." Folding her slender hand in his own, he again repeated, "I promise."

Amber smiled and her face lit up.

"I must warn you," she told him mischievously, "you must be prepared to spend some time in this country. Much of the story cannot be told, it must be shown." At his puzzled look she laughed aloud.

"You will understand better in time," she told him. She couldn't fail to note the relaxation of his big frame. For some reason he had been prepared to expect a fight from this golden girl. Instead she had agreed readily. The promise seemed a bit strange, yet in spite of himself, he could only be glad she had extracted it from him. Already, knowing Dr. Mackenzie's daughter, he could never bring public attention to anything that would reflect discredit on either her or her father.

"May I take you to dinner?" he asked a little uncertainly. He was still unsure of her response, but she only smiled again.

"That would be nice. Give me a little while to change out of my uniform."

"I'll be back in an hour," he promised, his eyes lighting. As he drove back to the Nez Perce Motel, he was humming under his breath. It had been a long time since he had taken a girl to dinner. His schedule was so irregular that it hadn't seemed worth the effort in most cases. Of course there had been girls in college, but since then he had been pretty much of a loner, content with his job.

He dressed carefully in his blue leisure suit and surveyed his rugged face with displeasure. Nothing very good about that homely mug. He couldn't realize there was strength and appeal in the very honest ruggedness he had just scowled at. Sam Reynolds had very little conceit, and none of it was about his looks.

When Amber opened the door he gasped. If she had been beautiful in her uniform, now she was exquisite. She had changed to a yellow dress, fitted to below the waist, then flaring into a wide swing. With it she wore a simple gold cross and a matching

31

wristwatch. She looked like an escaped ray of sunlight as she stood there in the doorway. Sam's usually dependable heart pounded. What was wrong with him, anyway? Even his college-day crushes had never brought this feeling of almost suffocation! Squaring his shoulders, he held Amber's matching yellow coat and helped her into his car.

He had taken the precaution of asking his new landlady where a good restaurant was located, and before long he and Amber were seated in a popular steak house. Amber's appetite amused him. Although tall, she was slender, and he wouldn't have thought she could eat like she did that night.

"It's the first real meal I've had time for since . . . since Dad died," she told him, forcing a mist back out of her eyes.

Sam understood then. She was probably half starved, what with the responsibility of the Crossroads Clinic the last week.

"I don't know when I've had better steak," he told her enthusiastically, and he meant it. This country whetted one's appetite. Sam had been busy that day too. Between calling Amber that morning and arriving at the clinic at four o'clock, he had spent several hours visiting various people who had known David Mackenzie. He had noticed that although all of them spoke highly of him, none seemed to either know or care anything about the doctor before he opened the Crossroads Clinic. He couldn't tell if it was ignorance on their parts or simply disinterest. Anyway, he had several pages of notes in his little pocket notepad.

During dinner Sam and Amber's conversation was carefully kept to surface issues. Neither cared to start anything where others might overhear or misunderstand. It was enough for Sam just to look at the lovely girl across from him. For a moment he allowed himself to think of what it would be like to have a real home, with a girl like this for a companion. He had seen enough of marriage to be a rather wary bachelor, but unconsciously Amber was weakening his defenses. The girl sensed some of this, and for a strange reason, was glad. She had never felt so alive in a man's presence before. She had dated many men, mostly doctors, while in training, and of course, there had always been Robert. But this man was different. His smile seemed to leave a glow in her heart.

Dinner was over too quickly for both, and Sam drove Amber home. They had decided not to open the subject of her father until the next day, which was Saturday. At one o'clock the clinic would close, with any emergencies referred into LaGrande. Amber had forgotten when she asked the woman with the burned arm to return the same time. She must call and ask her to come in earlier.

When they reached the Crossroads Clinic, Amber asked shyly, "Mr. Reynolds, would you think it strange if I asked you to do something for me?"

"Why, no." The man looked at her in surprise. "But would you call me Sam?"

"All right." She nodded. "Using a shortcut I know it is only a few minutes' drive out to my father's grave. Would you take me there, now? I haven't been since the funeral. Someday I will tell you why. But now I would like to go."

Silently he turned in the direction she pointed out, and a little while later they were standing before the headstone with its strange inscription.

What a difference since the first time he had stood there! Sam took his hat off — it seemed right to do so. For a long moment Amber gazed at the simple stone, then she motioned him to the car.

When they were back inside Sam asked very simply, "Why did you choose that particular inscription?"

Amber's answer was low, yet clear. "I didn't, Sam. My father chose it before he died — many years before." She lapsed into silence and did not speak again until they reached the Crossroads Clinic. Making no move to invite him in, she put her hand in his at the door.

"I will see you tomorrow at one," she said.

Sam's eyes looked directly into hers. "And you will tell me the story of your father?"

"I will start to tell you the story," she amended. "You must do the rest." Without another word she slipped into the house, leaving Sam on the doorstep, staring.

Brow knitted, he drove back to his cabin, glad there were still a few live coals. He felt exhilarated by the stinging cold night air, the story that lay ahead, and, yes, he admitted to himself, by Amber. He had never known a girl like her. She seemed unaware of her beauty, unspoiled by false modesty. She was simple, direct, yet he sensed a greatness in her. Had it come from her father? He mused until the fire went out, leaving him chilly. Yet in spite of his feeling there was an odd little nagging doubt. He couldn't quite get it.

Just as he went to sleep it returned. What was it she had said? Oh, yes: "I will start to tell you the story. . . . You must do the rest."

Unable to grasp her meaning, he impatiently thrust the words from him. Right now he had to sleep. He would find out tomorrow what she had meant. But a perverse spirit within seemed to say, Will you, Sam? Will you? As the clock struck twelve, Sam Reynolds was fast asleep.

But a few miles away, Amber lay sleepless, considering how best to start her father's story when the time came.

CHAPTER 3

Sam was awakened by the ringing of the telephone by the bedside. Reaching for it, he noticed how crisp and cold the weather had turned in the night. He enjoyed sleeping in a cold room, but this was something else! If he were to stay in this country for a while, and he intended to, it would be best to turn the thermostat a little higher.

Amber's voice came clearly over the phone.

"I just received a call from up the canyon and have to go out soon. Would you care to go with me? It will give us a chance to talk."

Gathering his senses Sam asked, "What about the clinic?"

"Robert said he will run out. His associate can handle anything that comes up. Besides, they aren't usually open on Saturdays."

"Robert?"

"Robert Meacham. He's an M.D. in

LaGrande." There was a trace of impatience in her voice. "Do you want to go or not?"

"I'll be there as soon as I can," Sam promised. The click of the receiver told him Amber was already gathering what she would need for the call. Staring at the phone for a moment, Sam shook himself and turned up the heat. In record time he was showered, shaved, and on his way. He hadn't had time for breakfast. Maybe Amber hadn't either, he thought. Well, anyway, when had a missed meal stopped him from a story? He grinned wryly. It wasn't the first and wouldn't be the last time, he was sure.

Amber was ready and waiting, a small medical case and a larger bag by her side. She nodded approvingly at his whipcord outfit and warm jacket. She herself wore a pants uniform today, covered with a fake-fur-lined carcoat and heavy mittens.

"Twenty-two degrees," she said, laughing as he gaped. Like so many others new to the country, the dryness of the climate was deceiving. He hadn't realized it was that cold.

State Highway 82 was beautiful. The frosty morning air seemed to crackle with anticipation. Golden tamaracks bordered the highway, and the Minam Canyon was beyond description. Never had Sam been so aware of nature's beauty. Was it because of his companion? Amber's hood had slipped back from her autumn-colored hair, and she seemed like a part of the surrounding countryside. As they traveled she explained. She usually came once a week to check on some of the older people who lived in small towns and out on ranches. It was hard for them to come in to the clinic.

Today's call had come from a remote sheep ranch in the rolling hills off the highway from Lostine. It would be a rough drive, but they would take it easy. There was no immediate hurry, the rancher had said. One of his boys had fallen from a tree and hurt an ankle. Their pickup truck had broken down, and the nearest neighbor had gone away for the weekend. If Miss Amber could please come, they would appreciate it.

"Do you get many calls like this?" Sam wanted to know.

Amber nodded. "Quite a few. Dad had a four-wheel drive jeep to get into some of the outlying areas in winter. He was the only doctor who could get through in almost any kind of weather." She paused and was silent for a long time, then went on. "I know you're anxious to know about my father. Last night I stayed awake a long time wondering just how to start."

Sam was amazed by her frankness. Nothing coy or flirtatious about her. It was a welcome relief from some of the women who worked on the *Star*.

Amber continued. "Since you said you had time, I decided to tell you the sequel before actually telling you the prologue, or the story."

Sam's puzzlement showed through his carefully determined look of understanding, and she laughed again.

"In other words, instead of starting at the time Dad left Portland Memorial and working up to his death, I am going to start in the present and work backward. That's why I want you to go with me on these callout trips whenever you can. If you see the end results of what Dad was trying to do, and talk with some of his patients, I hope you will find it easier to understand the beginning."

Sensing that she had said enough for a moment and how hard it was for her to talk of her father, Sam exclaimed, "Amber, I have never seen such country! Portland is beautiful, the drive up Columbia Gorge is spectacular, but the peace and stillness of this land of yours is beyond compare."

"Don't try to compare," she told him

quietly. "Comparisons are odious. It is like trying to decide whether oranges or bananas are best, when neither is anything at all like the other."

Sam glanced at her in appreciation. She had a knack of taking the simplest statement and making it fit exactly what he had been thinking.

Amber had been right about the road. When they left the state highway it was rough, but she was an excellent guide. Several turns later they wound around a high hill opening into a little valley. Ahead were several buildings, one a little apart from the rest. Amber directed him to park in front of the new home.

"Shall I come in with you?" Sam wanted to know.

Raising her eyebrows in surprise Amber said, "Of course. I wouldn't have you miss meeting the Carters for anything." Especially Crystal, she muttered under her breath, noticing that the lace window curtain was pulled aside, then hastily pushed back in place. By the time the front door was opened she knew who had been at the window. A ribbon was in the quickly combed blonde hair, and the smile on Crystal's face was much warmer than Amber had ever received from the girl.

"Do come in," she gushed. "Oh, Amber, we've just been waiting for you! You're always so much help, and . . . oh!" She put her hand to her mouth, green eyes widening in pretended surprise.

"I didn't see you had a stranger with you."

Sam looked completely bowled over by the greeting, Amber thought sourly. But then men never saw through Crystal. She was beautiful, Amber admitted to herself grudgingly. Small and dainty, Amber felt like an overgrown giant at five feet eight. Annoyance that she would care sharpened her tone. "Where's Billy?"

Crystal's red mouth made a little round circle of distress. "Oh, the poor baby! He just feels so badly." Quick tears filled her eyes.

Amber wanted to laugh. Never had she seen Crystal display any undue interest in her ten-year-old brother's welfare. Crystal led her to Billy's room and said, "I'll entertain your friend, Amber." With a sweet smile she placed her hand on Sam's arm, looking trustingly into his face.

"You know, I just couldn't bear all the horrid things Amber has to do for people." She shuddered delicately. "But then I'm not the strong type like she is. I so admire her, but then I'm far too sensitive to be like

42

Amber."

Pushing aside her fleeting irritation, Amber entered the room where Billy lay propped up in bed. His freckle-faced grin was a bit weak as he opened his eyes and looked at her.

"Hi, Billy," she said. "What seems to be the trouble?"

"Oh, I was climbing the apple tree and the durned thing broke," he told her disgustedly.

"What broke — the tree or your ankle?"

Billy grinned appreciatively. "Maybe both."

Deftly she felt the swollen ankle. It didn't seem to be broken. Just a bad sprain.

"That's good," she told Mrs. Carter approvingly, who had come in with fresh ice. "It will help reduce swelling."

"Will it be all right?" Billy's mother asked.

"As good as new in a day or so." Amber smiled. "But no more climbing trees for at least two weeks, young man!"

"Okay, Miss Amber." Billy's usual high spirits had risen at her diagnosis. When his mother had gone out of the room he added awkwardly, "I'm sorry about your dad."

Tears brimmed in Amber's eyes but she smiled at him. "It's all right, Billy. He had a good life."

The ten-year-old was serious. "Yeah, I know. He sure did a lot for all of us here." Something in his voice made Amber stop for a moment, then suddenly decide.

"Billy, I want you to meet someone. Someone I think you'll like." Crossing the room she called, "Sam, can you come in here for a moment?"

Sam's big frame almost filled the doorway. His open smile brought a quick response from Billy.

"You two should be good friends," Amber said. Something in her tone caused both of them to pause, but Sam stepped to the bed, holding out his brown hand.

"Any friends of Miss Mackenzie's are friends of mine."

"You bet!" Billy was quick to take his lead.

"Billy, Mr. Reynolds is interested in writing a story about my father. While I talk to your folks about how to fix up that ankle, maybe you can help him." Quietly she withdrew, leaving them alone.

Sam looked after her, astonished. This was the last thing he had expected. Noticing Billy's puzzled glance, he turned back to him.

"She's right. I work on the *Portland Star,* and we want to know about Dr. Mackenzie. Can you tell me about him?"

Billy's eyes glowed above the freckles.

"Sure. He was a swell guy. But what do you want to know?"

"Anything you want to tell me." Sam's reply was instantaneous.

For a long time Billy was quiet, then he began to talk. It was hard for him to get going — he didn't quite know where to start. But as he got warmed up Sam began to see David Mackenzie through a ten-year-old boy's eyes. Pure hero worship stood in the boy's face as he told how Dr. Mackenzie had worked for them all.

"I remember one time when my dog was sick. Dr. Mackenzie and Amber had come out to see how Grandma was. I was just a little kid then, but old Lad was a good dog. The vet in town had just given him a shot, then shook his head. He said there wasn't anything else to do. Lad was old. You couldn't make oldness well. Then Dr. Mackenzie came." Billy swallowed, and Sam could feel a matching lump in his throat.

"He found me out by the barn crying. I didn't want my dog to die. I had asked the preacher if dogs go to heaven and he said he didn't know. Well, Lad was good enough to go to any heaven there was. I knew that in a few weeks he had to die, but I sure was going to miss him. Wouldn't I ever see my dog again?"

Sam found himself leaning forward in his eagerness. Was Billy about to give a clue to that strange faith David Mackenzie had possessed?

Billy's voice was subdued as he went on. "When he came around the corner, there I was down on my hands and knees with Lad in my arms. He picked me up and wanted to know what the trouble was. 'Lad isn't going to heaven!' 'Who says he isn't?' 'I asked the preacher and he didn't know. What kind of God would make a dog, then let him die and not go to heaven? Lad is a good dog!'

"Dr. Mackenzie didn't say anything for a long time. Then he told me to always remember what he was going to say. I promised him I would." Billy looked earnestly at Sam.

"What did he tell you?" Sam asked gently.

"He said that every person had the right to believe what they wanted to but the kind of God he believed in was different than most folks' God. He said he thought that if God cared enough about Lad to make him live with me and be happy, then he cared enough about him that I shouldn't worry about Lad. Heaven was a mighty big place. Surely there must be a little corner in it for Lad."

Sam caught his breath. Billy was watching him intently.

"Do you think Dr. Mackenzie was right?" he asked anxiously. Sam could see that in spite of his faith in the doctor he needed to know others believed what he had been told, too. Almost without thinking he said, "Dr. Mackenzie was a very smart man, Billy. He should know."

Billy smiled, relief showing in his eyes. He finished the story:

"Lad lived about a week after that. When he died Dr. Mackenzie and Amber and I made a grave and put a cross on top of it. I felt bad, but not bad like I did before. Dr. Mackenzie showed me some of Mom's bulbs. They looked all dead, too, but he told me how after they were planted they came up in the spring and got to be flowers." He was silent for a long time again.

"I always think of Lad when I go to bring the sheep in and see flowers. Now I will think of Dr. Mackenzie too."

There was something in his voice that prevented Sam from further questions, a certain dignity in the small figure on the bed. Gripping his hand, Sam told him he would come back and visit when he could.

"Thanks for telling me about Dr. Mackenzie."

"It's all right." Billy shrugged off his seriousness. "Can I see your story when it's all done?"

Sam laughed, promising him he could, although it might be a long time in the future. The way he felt now, he had just begun to scratch the surface of the story of David Mackenzie. It would be a long time before he could put on paper the feelings he had experienced today.

Crystal was waiting outside Billy's door. She had wanted to go in, but Sam had closed the door behind Amber and she hadn't quite dared.

"I'm so glad you came," she told him. "It was precious of you to spend some time with Billy. I hope you'll come back to see us." There was an added emphasis on the us that Amber didn't fail to note.

"I'll be back," Sam told her, actually thinking of Billy. He wanted to spend more time with him.

Mr. Carter had come in from outdoors. Sam liked him at first sight. He was a strong man, obviously happy with his ranch and family. He asked Sam if he would like to see the place. After a glance at Amber to be sure they had time, Sam nodded. His tour of the ranch was quite an experience. The Carters had a fine flock of sheep, and the black-and-white border collies who helped with them were amazing. Sam couldn't believe how trained they were. All Mr. Carter had to do was raise a hand, and the dogs knew exactly what they were to do. He watched them bring a wandering ewe back to the flock, then turn the herd to the fenced-in pasture below the barn. Never had he seen such intelligent animals. One in particular with a white vest and plumy tail caught his eyes. She was a beauty.

"Lad's puppy," Mr. Carter explained. "We sold the others but kept this one from the last litter."

When they had waved good-bye to the Carters, Sam seemed lost in his thoughts. Amber hesitated to intrude, not knowing what had brought on his preoccupation. At last she ventured, "She's lovely, isn't she?" thinking of Crystal.

"She certainly is," Sam agreed. "I've never seen such an intelligent animal."

"Animal!" Amber gasped, then laughed until tears came to her eyes. Not for a million dollars would she let him know the relief she felt to know he had been thinking of the beautiful sheep dog when she had been secretly probing for a reaction to Crystal Carter!

"I'm sorry we didn't have time to stop and

49

see Grandma Carter," Amber told Sam regretfully. "But I promised Robert I'd get back as quickly as possible."

"It's all right," Sam assured her, while inside he was conscious of a cold feeling creeping over him. Who was this Dr. Robert Meacham she talked of so freely? Her left hand was ringless — surely she wasn't engaged?

Stop it! he told himself savagely. What is it to you if she is? It isn't reasonable for a girl like this one to not be spoken for. Besides, you didn't come here to fall in love, you came for a story. Keep it in mind! He felt better after the severe mental chastisement, and determined to stick to business. Yet as he gained Amber's promise to show him something of the surrounding country the next day, his unruly heart beat fast.

If Amber had known his thoughts perhaps she would not have felt a curious sense of defeat when he had dropped her at the clinic. Why couldn't Crystal have been gone today, as she usually was? Impatiently she glared at her sun-gold image in the mirror. Why wasn't she blonde, with green eyes? Amber had no way of knowing that her bright coloring was what attracted Sam. Crystal's green eyes and blonde hair couldn't hold a candle to Amber in his eyes.

CHAPTER 4

The chief of the *Star* riffled through his morning mail impatiently. It had been a week since Sam had gone to LaGrande — he ought to be hearing from him. He didn't expect much in the way of results yet, but at least Sam could drop a note! Ah! Here it was, a thick letter. Hastily scanning the other mail, he buzzed his secretary.

"No interruptions until I ring again," he told her.

"Yes, sir." Her tone was surprised. In the five years she had been with the *Star* this was the first time the chief had closed his door. Usually anyone who wanted to see him just dropped in. Shrugging her shoulders, she closed the door behind her. The chief knew what he was doing. Still, she was a bit curious as to the reason. Gossip had it the chief had sent Sam Reynolds on some special assignment and she had noted his letter when she sorted the mail.

Don Baker ripped open the envelope eagerly. Settling back he began to read.

Dear Chief,

Sorry I haven't written sooner, but it has taken me all week to get my thoughts collected enough to know where to start. First of all, I wouldn't have missed this assignment for anything. The country itself is enough to keep you walking around with your mind expanded — the color is fantastic. Red, yellow, gold, amber — oh, yes, Amber!

Chief, did you forget that David Mackenzie had a little daughter at the time he and his wife left Portland? A little girl named Amber? Well, she isn't a little girl anymore. She's a beautiful woman, who matches her name. Everything about her is amber. Name, personality, naturally curly hair, eyes. She shines! People love her wherever she goes, I've found out that, even in the short time I've been here. I have never known anyone who gets so much out of life even though she has just lost her father. Whatever it is you thought her father had, and I'm beginning to believe he really did have something, it has evidently been transmitted to his daughter. She is a radiant human being, and thoroughly unspoiled.

So far, Amber hasn't told me why her father left Portland. But she has taken me with her to visit many of his patients. Most of them are on small farms, some on sheep ranches, on back roads, in valleys, on hilltops. *Yet not one of them has anything but the highest praise for David Mackenzie!* Although I am no nearer his reason for leaving Portland Memorial, I am firmly convinced there was nothing dishonorable about his decision. Only a dedicated doctor could win the confidence and love of the people the way he evidently did.

I don't know how to explain this feeling, but you know I'm not one to take things on face value only — they have to be based on some pretty hard facts. Yet I have never felt more strongly regarding anything. Dr. Mackenzie's memory is untainted in the minds of these people.

Let me give you an example of what he and Amber have done for this country.

When Amber returned from nurse's training to work with her father, the whole area rejoiced. We went to see Grandma Carter, a little old lady who lives in the rolling foothills. Even though she is over eighty she refuses to live with her son and his family. For a time there was a big hassle about her being there alone. The family came to Dr. Mackenzie and talked with him about it. They felt it was too uncertain, what with bad weather and all, for her to be out there alone. It's about five miles from their own ranch and in winter is hard to get to.

Dr. Mackenzie promised to talk to "Granny," as the whole country calls her. She is a little white-haired lady, taught school locally for many years, and now delights in visits from the kids, their kids, and their grandkids. No one knew what he said to her, but she went to her son and made a compromise. She would stay in her own place from spring through fall, but when winter rolled around, would consent to move back to her son's home. In fact, I helped move her this last week. She really appreciated it. She asked me how she could repay me, and without thinking I blurted out:

"Tell me how Dr. Mackenzie convinced you to leave your cabin for the winters." I felt rather ashamed as her piercing blue eyes looked through me, then softened into a twinkle.

"Promise not to tell my son?"

I promised solemnly.

"He accused me of being selfish."

I must have gasped my amazement. No one has ever been more unselfish than Granny Carter, who is loved by everyone.

"He was right," she said. "I didn't want to impose on my son's family by living with them. So I insisted on living in my own little house, all alone. Meanwhile all winter long they worried about me, wondering how I was until they could get me shoveled out. When I realized what I was doing to them, I gave in."

There was a contented look on her face as she added, "I'm glad."

Chief, this is only one example of what this remarkable man has accomplished. I could tell you of his goodness and wisdom to one little boy and his dog, or about the welfare family without hope, or a dozen others. But I will hold off on those stories.

For now I think it will be enough to assure you that from everything I can find out, David Mackenzie was an outstanding man. His daughter Amber is

continuing his work. Will write again
soon,

Sam

Baker folded his letter carefully and
tucked it away in a bottom drawer. As he
rang for his secretary, the relief in his face
was evident. Again she wondered what news
Sam Reynolds's letter had contained, but
didn't ask. The chief began dictating immediately and the day continued its usual
hectic pace.

There was no way those around him could
know what was going on inside their chief.
He maintained his usual calm in the midst
of chaos, but between visitors and the
constantly ringing telephone an inner voice
was shouting, David Mackenzie was all
right! He didn't cut and run because of
some unseemly conduct.

That night when the chief had gone home
to his mansion on the hillside overlooking
Portland and the Columbia River, he stood
at the great window watching the city lights
below.

"I never knew how much I wanted to
believe him innocent," he said aloud. It was
true. A great weight had rolled from him.
He felt ten years younger. If he had been a
man of faith, he would have knelt and

thanked God. As it was he let his emotion overflow by turning up a symphony presentation on the stereo, letting the music swell through him. After a time he hunted out an old scrapbook and reread the clippings from so many years ago. Suddenly deciding, he placed them in a large mailing envelope and addressed it to Sam. He would look up the zip code in the morning and mail the whole batch from the office. It should help Sam in his mission.

The chief smiled to himself. Yes, it was a mission he had sent Sam on, not just an assignment. At first it would have been enough to know David Mackenzie had lived his life out according to the personal standards he had set. Now that was no longer sufficient. Don Baker wanted to know every bit of information about his old friend, what had made him tick, what set him apart from other men.

Seizing a pen he dashed off a note:

Keep up the good work — stay until all information possibilities are exhausted. You can't know what this means to me.

His signature was a bold scrawl below.

Across the miles to the east Sam laughed at

the note. It was so like his chief! Then he sobered. He knew the chief was depending on him for a lot more than an average story called for. Although he believed the things he was learning, could Don Baker ever really know how much David Mackenzie had done? A glint came to his eye as a fresh possibility crept to mind. He would get all he could, then insist the chief come meet those same people Amber was introducing him to now. It was the only way.

Sam frowned. Although it was true he was seeing what Amber called the "results," he felt himself no closer to the original mystery of why her father had left Portland in the first place! Every person he met was more than willing to share what he had done for them, yet a strange quiet prevailed about Dr. Mackenzie's past.

Several times he had broached the subject, sometimes hinting, often asking right out. No one took the bait. An original clam couldn't have been more close-mouthed than some of these people! Sam felt a rising irritation. Why wouldn't these people talk? He had even tried a detour by asking several what the inscription on Dr. Mackenzie's tombstone meant — "accepted the Cross-roads Calling." No one seemed to know anything more than that it was what the doctor had chosen many years before. Or maybe they knew but wouldn't tell him. Even though he had been accepted because of Amber, Sam realized he would have to prove himself to these people before they would have confidence in him. Amber told him once a Portland reporter had come to the area for a story and pictures. On returning to his newspaper, he wrote an article ridiculing the simple way of life, referring to the people as "quaint," "behind-the-times," and so on. No wonder they were a little reluctant to expose their hardworking way of life to a stranger!

Sam had learned in the short time he spent among them that there were no finer people anywhere. Those who had shared with those who had not. Especially in some of the outlying areas, there were still old-fashioned "work trades" at harvest time. There was a neighborliness, bordering on nosiness, yet filled with a real concern for each other that he had never known in Portland. Amber told him the small-town gossip could be annoying, but he only smiled. Working on a newspaper was the last place to be free of gossip, and he sensed in this country more interest than malicious-ness.

It was early November now. The days had

passed rapidly as Amber took Sam to the different areas. He loved Wallowa Lake best of all. The jutting bars covered with trees, many of the golden leaves drifted in piles underneath now, the clearness of the water. Often while Amber was busy elsewhere Sam would go up Minam Canyon and on to the lake. Since he had been away from Portland a growing desire to be more than just an excellent reporter had filled him. Alone in the outdoors he felt inspired to really do something with his writing talent. There was so much trash being printed these days, if he could only write a book that would be inspirational, something to make people's lives a little happier, a little better.

One nippy morning when he awakened there was about an inch of snow on the ground. After dressing warmly, he headed for the lake. He wanted to see it in all its garb. He stopped for a moment at a favorite spot just outside Joseph, the monument to Chief Joseph and his people. More than ever he could understand how those people so long ago fought bitterly to keep the land. And what a land! Snowcapped mountains vied with stark branches now iced in white for his attention. The lake was still, reflecting faithfully the trees and sky above until it was difficult to determine where reality began and image ended.

"I am completely contented," Sam told a giant tree. He stood on a small bridge crossing a burbling mountain stream. Snow-capped rocks stood up in the swirling water, the banks were lined with trees. What a fantastic place! It was all he could do to tear himself away, but it was starting to snow in earnest now and he had many miles back to his lodging.

There was something in the air that day Sam knew he would never forget. The stillness, for one thing. The beautiful deer stepping cautiously into the edge of the road, unafraid as he slowed and let her cross. The whiteness, clean and pure. So different from the rush of the city. If only Amber could have been with him, Sam regretted, then he caught himself up with a sheepish grin. No doubt she had seen this very spot a hundred times. Her work took her all over. He wondered how she would react now that the Crossroads Clinic was sold. It had been the only practical thing to do, yet it had hurt her to sell, he knew that. It was good she had held off. The idea of a nursing home had been unappealing. She had waited, and Dr. Meacham had bought it. He had a partner who would keep regular hours there, and Amber would take over as many calls out from the clinic as she could handle. It seemed an ideal arrangement, and she was very grateful.

Sam ground his teeth. Although he liked Robert Meacham personally, he was jealous of him, too. It seemed he had everything that would attract Amber. They had medicine in common, both were settled to country living. What did Sam have to offer? Life in Portland? It was a beautiful city, but Amber loved the country. Then too, if Sam looked for work locally, there wouldn't be much choice. Unless I do decide to write a book, he added mentally, feeling the thrill within him.

I'll do it! he vowed, with only the swish-swish of the windshield wipers to witness his decision. I'll stay here long enough to write a book, one that will make the world a little better place to live in. It would take work, and time. He knew that. Then, too, there was no guarantee of success. Strangely enough, that didn't matter. Sam knew he could get by for quite a while on what he had saved. Once his decision was made, he could hardly wait to tell Amber. Then he thought, No, I'll surprise her. It's better not to raise hopes in any of my friends with big plans. I won't tell anyone, except maybe the chief. I'll have to ask for extended time here.

Excitement filled him. Why not find out what strange happenings had led to David Mackenzie's arrival at the Crossroads Clinic and use them in his story? Never had he been filled with such anticipation. As soon as he reached the Nez Perce Motel he grabbed his typewriter and started writing. Nothing concrete, just impressions, ideas, bits and pieces of things he had heard. He forgot about lunch and would have worked straight through dinner but the light from the window faded and he realized the time.

Starved but content, he covered the type-writer, reread the pages, and changed clothes. A thrill shot through him: the mate-rial was good. Now if he could only make David Mackenzie come alive! Thoughtfully he considered various plots and approaches, only to reject them all. If his hero was to be based on Dr. Mackenzie, then he would have to wait until he knew more about him. In the meantime there was the Box Social, and it was time for him to pick up Amber.

"A Box Social?" he had said when Amber invited him to go. "I didn't know anyone still had such a thing."

"You'll like it," she told him, mischief in her eyes. "The Wallowa country has some of the best cooks in the world, and each vies with the other to make the most tasteful and tasty dinner imaginable! Save your appetite, you'll need it!"

He chuckled now, thinking of her words. He certainly had followed her advice! He could eat a bear. He had tried to find out how her box would be decorated, but she shook her head firmly. It wasn't fair to give things away, he was told emphatically. In spite of all his wheedling she had remained firm.

"Robert asked too," she commented innocently. "I wouldn't tell him either."

A pang of gladness mixed with irritation shot through him. Robert Meacham was an ever-present threat to his peace of mind these days, but he knew he had no right to feel this way. Nevertheless he was glad he would be the one to take Amber to the party tonight. It would be the first social event they had attended together. He was also glad that the proceeds would go to getting better fire equipment for the small town where it was being held. It seemed just another link in the concern he had felt of the people who lived there, and which was slowly but surely chaining him to this country with invisible bonds.

CHAPTER 5

The party was in full swing when Sam and Amber arrived at the school gymnasium. It was amazing how many had braved the threat of a storm to attend.

Amber explained, "It's always like this." She brushed snowflakes from her coat. "Everyone from Elgin to Joseph supports these community activities — including Lostine," she said, nodding to the Carters, who had just come in. Billy's sprain was a thing of the past and the whole family was present.

"Why, hel-lo there!" Crystal's voice was as honey smooth as the shining hair cascading to the low-cut neckline of her ruffled taffeta gown.

"How quaint," she told Amber, lightly touching the old-fashioned lilac dimity dress sprigged with tiny nosegay clusters of yellow flowers.

"Isn't that Granny's?"

Amber's expressive eyes scanned Crystal.

"Yes, we thought it would be fun to wear old-time gowns."

"Granny must have forgotten to tell me," Crystal said, smugly aware of the sharp contrast between her own striking appearance and the simple cottons surrounding her. Giving Amber no chance to reply, she linked her arm in Sam's, green eyes glowing.

"Come see Granny," she urged. "She really has taken a shine to you — her expression, not mine." Sam started to protest but Dr. Meacham stepped to Amber's side at that moment.

"Robert!" There was pleasure in the girl's tone. "I was afraid you wouldn't make it after that emergency." Seeing how intently she was listening to Dr. Meacham's report, Sam allowed Crystal to lead him away.

"They're the same as engaged, you know," Crystal whispered confidingly, leaning close. Sam's heart sank but he maintained a cool interest.

"I wondered if it had been announced yet."

"Oh, mercy no! Don't say anything about it. I really shouldn't have mentioned it but then you're with Amber so much I figured you'd already know." She gazed up at him

66

as though her dearest wish was about to be granted just as Amber glanced across the room. Sam caught the quick look flaring in her eyes before she turned back to Dr. Meacham. Taking a step toward her, he was stopped in place by Tom Carter's hearty shout:

"Hear ye, hear ye!" The buzz of conversation died as he stepped behind a long table laden with boxes of every size, shape, and decoration imaginable. Delicious odors enticed the crowd to the rows of folding chairs arranged facing the laden table.

"The rules are simple," he announced. "By popular demand" — he was interrupted by a wave of laughter — "I have been selected to auction off the boxes. Now the ladies, bless their hearts, have spent all day cooking up what's in these packages. It's up to us men to reach down in our pocketbooks and dig out those old musty dollars! We're not just buying a dandy supper, but the privilege of eating with some of the prettiest gals in northeastern Oregon! And it's all for a good cause!"

He picked up a beribboned box and sniffed.

"Smells like Aunt Sadie's fried chicken. Might buy this one myself!"

Bids flew thick and fast. Tom Carter was a

master auctioneer, interspersing the bidding with his own witty comments. He had a special introduction for every box.

As the evening wore on and the boxes dwindled, Sam and Robert warily eyed the remaining ones. They had both made token bids but nothing serious. Each was determined to buy Amber's box, but so far neither her nor Crystal's had been sold. Then Tom held up a beautiful box wrapped in lilac and tied with yellow ribbon. Sam's heart beat fast. It must be Amber's! Engaged or not, he meant at least to buy her box and have dinner with her, but the set look on Robert's face gave fair warning he was equally determined.

"One dollar." "Two dollars." "Five dollars." Most of the other boxes had gone from five to ten dollars. Only Sam and Robert were still in the bidding at fifteen dollars, then Sam called out,

"Twenty-five."

Silence greeted his statement, then Granny Carter spoke in her drawling tones, "Now, boys, I sure am flattered you all want to eat supper with me, but that's high enough even for my best wild blackberry pie. Bidding's over!"

The crowd gasped. They had all been sure the box was Amber's. Amid loud cheering

Sam joined in the laugh at his expense and gallantly bowed to Granny, claiming both her and the box.

"Not guilty!" she protested, blue eyes twinkling. "Amber made me do it!" Sam only grinned. Amber's look of approval at his courteous acceptance of the situation had not been lost on him.

Tom Carter held up another box, this time decorated as an American flag. After much spirited bidding Robert claimed it and led Crystal away.

There was only one box left before the auctioneer, and it was a beauty! The owner had cleverly taken a willow basket, lined it with birch bark, and decorated it with moss and tiny polished rocks. The basket alone was worth a good price, and from inside peeked plastic-wrapped fried chicken, cups of potato salad, strawberry tarts, pickles, olives, and great wedges of chocolate cake.

"Aw, gee." Billy Carter's heart was in his eyes. "I'd sure like to have that!" He had bid several times before but always lost out to a higher bidder.

Tom Carter looked down kindly at his son. "How much money do you have?"

"Two dollars." Ten-year-old pride showed through the rusty freckles. "Been saving up for tonight."

"Sold!" Amber stepped forward. "That is my basket and I claim the right to auction it off myself." Billy's face lighted up.

"Really?" He grabbed the basket with one hand, Amber with the other, and proudly led her to a table. Sam saw the envious glances following them. Not a young man was present who wouldn't have liked to trade places with Billy, yet not one word of protest was made. Amber's small act of kindness had only endeared herself to them even more.

What a girl! Throughout the delicious basket supper Sam couldn't keep his eyes off her. Had she learned her kindness, her gentleness, from her father? It was one of the things he meant to find out. He didn't realize how expressive his face was until Granny chuckled aloud.

"If I wasn't an old lady I'd be miffed. Seems you ought to pay more attention to the girl whose box you wanted so badly!" Her sharp eyes noted the dull red around Sam's collar as he grinned at her, not minding she had guessed his secret.

"Go after her, son. You don't look like a man who would let a few obstacles stand in your way," she added, nodding toward Dr. Meacham and Crystal.

Sam met Granny's clear eyes squarely. "I

hear Amber's engaged."

Granny snorted. "Not so you'd notice it! I've known her for a long time. Sure, she's fond of Robert, but she's not in love with him. They grew up together; sometimes she feels obligated because of their long friendship. But when Amber falls in love that will be it. She's a one-man woman. None of this on-again, off-again stuff for her. It will be for keeps. No reason why you shouldn't see if it could be you."

Sam's heart began to pound with hope and he leaned closer.

"You really mean . . ." He was interrupted by Crystal's plaintive voice.

"Granny, you've monopolized our visitor long enough. I want to talk with him. Besides, they're calling for squares for the square dancing."

"I can't square dance," Sam protested, but it was useless. In spite of himself he was pushed and pulled into place by a laughing crowd determined to show him he could. Doing the best he could he was soon lost in a maze of "do-si-do," "Allemand left" until Amber took pity on him. When a "change partners" was announced she appeared at his side.

"Let's sit this one out," she told him, her flushed face rosy above the dainty dress.

Leading him to the row of chairs, they watched the happy group in their ever-changing patterns. Crystal's long blonde hair and out-of-place green dress was conspicuous among the sets, and Amber felt a pang at the arch smiles she cast their way each time her square formed in the area where they sat.

Sam was much too dazed to make the most of his opportunity, and before he could do more than enjoy just sitting with Amber, Billy joined them.

"They need another couple, Amber," he said shyly. "You wouldn't want to dance with me, would you?"

"Why, Billy, of course! I was wondering if you were going to buy my basket and then not even dance with me!" They sailed off, taking their places in a new square forming.

Within moments Crystal had dropped from her square and sought out Sam.

"I have something to talk over with you," she said. "Come out here where it's quieter." With a backward glance at Amber, who pretended not to see them go, Sam followed the blonde girl into an empty classroom nearby.

Crystal's plan tumbled out. She knew he was a writer and needed a quiet place to do his work. Sam started. He had told no one of his determination to do a book! Then he realized Crystal must be referring to his assignment for the *Star.* As he listened to her scheme, in spite of seeing that the girl had an ulterior motive, he was enchanted.

"I just told Granny how a man like you mustn't be disturbed when you're trying to work. It must be an awful nuisance to drive 'way up here in this country clear from LaGrande now that the weather's getting bad. The roads will be icy and we get a lot of snow some winters. If you don't mind being snowed in now and then for a day until we can get you dug out, Granny would be proud to have you use her cabin for the winter. She always worries about it when she's with us." She laughed a bit condescendingly.

"I really don't see why. After all, if it's all snowed in, what can harm it? But anyway, she'd be glad for you to live there until spring, if you're going to be in this part of the country that long?" There was a prying note to her question.

Not committing himself, Sam replied, "Crystal, that would be great! It is a little hard to be so far away from all the small towns when I need to know about them."

Crystal clasped her hands together in joy. "Oh, won't it be fun! We're your nearest neighbor, you know!" She blushed at Sam's amusement.

"Well, in this country, five miles isn't so far!"

Sam's imagination took fire. If he could be alone, sometimes snowbound, what couldn't he do with his writing! Anyway, it would give him fair opportunity to see just how much he could accomplish. It would be beautiful, too. He could almost see the long drifts hanging from tree branches, the icicles on the shed roof as Crystal painted the cabin in glowing terms.

"You'll have to learn to use snowshoes," she told him. "And be sure you have chains as well as snow tires. We have a cat for clearing if it's a real hard winter."

Sam couldn't have cared less about contact. As long as there was plenty of food in the house and wood for Granny's fireplace, he would be happy.

"How soon can you come?" Crystal wanted to know. A strange glow in her green eyes made Sam hesitate for a moment. Then he called himself crazy for thinking she was up to something and forced back his suspicion. After all, she had fixed things so he could have freedom to write, hadn't she? A rush of gratitude swept over him and impulsively he leaned over and kissed her smooth cheek.

"You're a dear, Crystal," he told her.

"Sorry to break up this touching scene, but the party is over." Amber stood in the doorway. The light note of amusement in her voice covered her inner rage at the sight of the kiss. She had no way of knowing it meant nothing whatsoever to Sam — all she saw was the triumphant look Crystal gave her.

"Oh, Amber, isn't it wonderful!" Crystal gushed, oblivious of Sam's embarrassment. "Sam is coming to live in Granny's cabin and do his writing there!"

Amber gave her a cool smile and said shortly, "Congratulations, Sam. Now if you don't mind" — she motioned to the doorway where Tom Carter had appeared — "Mr. Carter wants to lock up."

The silence in Sam's car was in sharp contrast to the laughing evening they had just spent. Sam was aware he had inadvertently put himself in a bad light with Amber. A few miles down the road he attempted to explain.

"Amber, about that kiss . . ." The girl looked at him in apparent surprise.

"Kiss? Oh, yes, you were kissing Crystal, weren't you?" She laughed tolerantly, a

75

triumph of will over emotion. "Don't worry about it, Sam, Crystal won't sue you for breach of promise or anything. She's used to all the fellows being after her." Her understanding tone made Sam feel like a small boy caught stealing sheep.

Feeling his face flush in the darkness he blundered on. "It didn't mean anything, I was just . . . that is . . ."

Amber's laugh cut through his explanation.

"Goodness, you don't have to explain to me! It's nothing at all to me whom you kiss or when!" Her slight sarcasm effectively silenced Sam until they reached her doorstep, then fury at the awkward position he had been placed in came over him. Losing his head for a moment he reached out and before Amber could protest, he gathered her in his arms and kissed her squarely on the mouth.

A ringing slap left pain in his left cheek. Amber's eyes were filled with tears of rage.

"Just what do you think you're doing? First Crystal, now me! Well, let me tell you something, Mr. Portland Reporter, leave me out of your fun and games! This may be a modern world but I still believe a kiss should mean something, not be an expected thank you at the end of a date!" With a mighty shove of the door she went in, slamming it hard behind her.

Sam stood on the porch, his heart sinking. In a moment of loss of self-control he had forfeited the wonderful friendship he and Amber had begun. Miserable, he climbed in his car and went back to the motel, calling himself every name he could think of. He had known from the first she was a different kind of girl. Granny Carter had confirmed it. Now he had gone and done this! It was a long time before Sam Reynolds slept.

It was just as well he could not have seen Amber after he left. Tears of helpless fury flowed down her face.

"Well! So that's the kind of man he is! Good thing you found out before you began to let him creep into your heart! At least Robert would never force himself on a girl, especially after her seeing him with another girl less than an hour before!" she stormed to herself until some of the bitterness was gone. When she regained some of her composure, she prepared for bed, rejoicing she had found out in time. But the lump of misery inside raised the question she could not honestly answer: Is it in time? Is it?

CHAPTER 6

There were dark circles under Amber's big eyes the next morning. She had spent a sleepless night, trying to convince herself that she hated Sam Reynolds. What right had he to come and stir up trouble? She pushed aside the memory of the happy hours they had spent as he went with her on the rounds. She forced herself to discount the genuine admiration she had seen in his eyes at the deft bandaging of a wound or the gentle way she used with the tiny patients. It all seemed meaningless in the face of that triumphant gleam from Crystal's green eyes the night before.

"Cat!" Somehow saying it aloud helped Amber feel better. Funny, it had never irritated her before when Crystal captured the attention of the male portion of the countryside.

"I'm not going to think about it any more," Amber promised her mirrored reflection as she brushed the golden-brown hair until it shone. She smiled wryly. Talking to herself, now. That must be a sign of something or other.

She gazed around her little home with affection, gratitude toward Robert filling her. When Robert bought the clinic and installed his partner, Dr. Mitchell, they had both insisted Amber keep her own living quarters.

"Goodness, they wouldn't even begin to hold the Mitchell tribe," the doctor had told her, eyes twinkling. He had five children and needed the space of the old ranch house nearby he was remodeling. So Amber had remained in the little home she and her father had shared for so many years. She was too busy to ever be lonely, yet sometimes she wished she had a pet. A dog would be hard to keep but it would be nice to have a cat to purr on the hearth during the long evenings. As if her wish had conjured one up, she heard the outside door to the clinic open and a faint meow. Eyes widening, she rushed to the waiting room.

Robert Meacham looked up sheepishly from the big red bow he was tying on the golden-striped tiger cat. "Caught in the act!"

"Oh, Robert, what a beauty!" Amber had forgotten she had once mentioned she wanted a yellow-gold cat for her hearth.

Now this one, little more than a kitten, looked up appealingly, his white face contrasting sharply with his beautiful amber-colored hair.

"He seemed to match you," the doctor told her laughingly, affection in his eyes. "He's all weaned and housebroken. He won't be a problem."

"He's darling!" The delighted girl cuddled the little animal closer, his fur almost the same color as her own short curly hair.

"You'll have to name him, Robert, since you found him."

Robert looked pleased. "Well . . ." he considered the little cat seriously.

"We could call you Cuddles, but that's no name for the dignity you must learn as an R.N.'s kitty. Then there's plain old Cat, but you have to do better than that. Let's see. I know . . . we'll call you Tawny."

Amber clutched the kitten closer. "That's perfect! Oh, Robert, how can I thank you enough?" She leaned across to him, eyes shining, and gave him a sisterly kiss. Neither of them had noticed the door behind Robert opening until Sam Reynolds spoke from the threshold, his voice an exact replica of Amber's the night before.

"Sorry to break up this touching scene, but I just stopped by to say good-bye for a while. I'm all packed and on my way to Granny Carter's cabin. I'll be in touch with you, Miss Mackenzie. Have a happy Thanksgiving, both of you." He touched the brim of his newly acquired wide hat and was gone.

Amber stared after him in consternation. Of all the times to be interrupted! That kiss had only been a warm expression of gratitude, but how could he know that? Tears filled her eyes as she thought of the stiffness of his back as he marched out the door.

"So that's it." Robert's voice was tender, yet filled with newly awakened knowledge. "You're in love with him."

Amber was recalled to the present by the pain in his voice. A fresh wave of tears flooded her eyes. Unable to protest, she mutely looked up at this good friend of the years, noticing the tiny lines of suffering at the corner of his mouth.

"I'm sorry," she faltered.

"Don't be, Amber. I guess I've always known you weren't in love with me, and that someday this would happen. But why him? He will take you away from the Wallawas, back to the city. It's his life. Can you live like that?"

Amber shook her head. "I don't know, but

there's no reason to think he — he even cares."

"He cares." Robert's voice was grim. "But remember this, Amber. If you ever need me, I'll be waiting. Just like I always have been." There was bitterness in his tone.

"I wish I did care the way you want me to!" Amber was sincere, the doctor could see that. For the first time since Sam's departure he smiled, a little crooked, but still a smile.

"Don't worry about it, Amber. Things will be the way they are meant to be. Remember? Your father taught you that. Don't forget the motto for living he gave both of us — 'follow the Crossroads Calling.' " There was a faraway look of remembrance in the glance they shared out the window in the direction of the little cemetery.

The silence was broken by a plaintive meow, reminding them that Tawny was anxious for more breakfast than Robert had given him before bringing him out to Amber. In a few moments he was happily lapping a saucer of milk on the kitchen floor.

"We should have named him Piggy from the way he eats!" Robert stooped to stroke the soft fur, then added in the tone a mother uses to her child on the first day of school, "Now mind your manners so the nice lady will take good care of you. Don't track mud on her nice clean floor, and don't leave wet pawprints on the furniture. Be a good little kitty and she'll give you a good home."

The utter ridiculousness of his solemn admonitions to the cat was too much for Amber. Sinking down onto the floor next to Tawny, she burst into laughter, releasing the strain she had felt from their former conversation. Robert joined in wholeheartedly, his disappointment for a moment laid aside. But when he rose to go he reminded gently, "I haven't given up, Amber. I've loved you too many years for that."

For a moment Amber was tempted to throw herself in his arms and tell him she would marry him. He was so kind, so good! Life would always be pleasant with him, safe, secure. She could remain here in the beautiful country she loved so well. There would be no danger of ever having to give up her beloved work, for they would work together the way she and Dad had done. And she did love him . . . not in the thrilling excitement of the moments with Sam, but with a steady warmth.

Robert must have guessed her thoughts to some extent for he shook his head.

"No, Amber. I don't want a wife without all her love, not just warm affection. It would be wrong for us both."

She extended her hands wordlessly, and after a quick pressure, Robert too was gone, leaving Amber to finish feeding the kitten and get into her uniform before Dr. Mitchell and the day's work arrived.

It was a busy day, too much so for any personal problems to intrude. There was a call from the Kincaids near Summerville, a tiny village off the main highway north of LaGrande. Sally May's baby was on its way and Mark had gone to town earlier with their station wagon. Could they come?

Shaking his head at such poor planning, Dr. Mitchell threw his hands up in the air. Never would he get used to people who wanted to have babies at home rather than in the hospital.

"Well, they didn't exactly plan for the baby to come two weeks early," Amber reminded as they hurriedly put together what they would need. "Besides, it's her third. It won't be as bad as the first." Only too well did Amber and Dr. Mitchell remember Sally May's first. It was the same time of year, only there had been an unexpected blizzard. Even Dr. Mackenzie's jeep had given out half a mile from the house and while the girl was trying frantically to hold back the baby, Amber and her father came the last part of the trip on snowshoes. When they arrived, it was to find a brand-new baby all delivered, wrapped, and nestled close to its mother!

"Sorry," the young husband apologized with a smile. "She just couldn't hold off any longer!"

Dr. Mackenzie and Amber exchanged a long look, then burst out laughing. The mother, baby, and father were all doing fine.

"There's one thing about having a ranch," Dr. Mackenzie told his daughter on the trek back to the jeep. "Even the youngsters know all about lambing time and the like. Then when an emergency arises they can handle it. Of course Mrs. Kincaid, Mark's mother, was the real help. She's practically a midwife in her own right. Never lost a baby."

Dr. Mitchell smiled now as Amber repeated her father's words. Despite his disapproval of some of the old-time ways, he still had a strong admiration for the self-reliant people he served.

It didn't take long to arrive at the Kincaids'. The rugged jeep had no trouble with the snowy lane, and all was in readiness when they arrived. Again Mrs. Kincaid was present, and her knowledge and skill in having things set up for them saved a great deal of time. In less than two hours a brand-new baby girl had joined the two little brothers in the family.

Amber oiled the tiny being and wrapped her in blankets warmed from the fireplace, wondering for a moment how it would be to hold a little one of her own in her arms. What if she and Sam . . . She fiercely thrust the thought aside, a rich blaze of color staining her face, scorning herself for the idea.

In a few moments Sally May had her new daughter beside her. Even Dr. Mitchell had to admit they looked fully at home. With Mrs. Kincaid there to look after the family, Sally May would get the best of care. Just now she had called the neighbor who had taken the two small boys when it became evident a new baby was on its way. Her firm voice brooked no arguments.

"Thanks anyway, but no help is needed. If you can bring the boys back this afternoon we will be fine."

Mrs. Kincaid turned from the phone, a smile in her dark eyes. "We'd be proud if you could stop by again, Miss Amber."

"Of course," Amber agreed. Turning to Sally May she asked, "What are you going to name her?"

A shy smile greeted her question. "Would you mind . . . that is, Mark and I would like to name her Amber Lee."

Amber was touched. "I think that's a beautiful name." She knew Lee was Mark's mother's name, and turned to the older woman. "With a name like that she will be all right, won't she!"

There was pleasure in Mrs. Kincaid's face. "Yes, she certainly will. But mostly because of how Mark and Sally May will raise her."

When Dr. Mitchell and Amber left, the doctor said, "One of the most rewarding parts of medicine."

Amber agreed quietly. "Yes, what can be more beautiful than a new life coming into a home where it has been longed for and planned for?"

"Tired?" Dr. Mitchell asked. "Let's stop at the ranch and see what Nell has cooked up. She was baking bread today. Maybe it's still warm."

Amber's spirits brightened. There was no one she thought any more of than Nell Mitchell. Too busy with her children and gigantic remodeling project for much social life, she welcomed Amber's infrequent visits with pleasure. She loved the girl like a younger sister and was always glad to see her.

Today Dr. Mitchell was right. Her home-made bread was just out of the oven, a big pot of soup simmering on the back of the stove. Although it had been planned for supper she didn't mind a bit. She could always make something else if they ate it for dinner!

There wasn't much time to visit. The trip to the Kincaids' had taken up much of the day and Dr. Mitchell had a few other patients coming in that afternoon.

"Come for Thanksgiving," Nell invited warmly. "Robert will be out. It will be almost like old times."

Remembering the many Thanksgivings she and her father had spent with the Mitchells, Amber agreed. It would be hard without him, but she didn't want to spend the day alone. She could have gone to the Carters, but with Sam there, it was best to stay away. Let Crystal enjoy the day with him. She was ashamed of herself for the thought, and made up for it by promising, "I'll bring my new little kitty out if it's all right — I think your children will want to see him." Nell Mitchell didn't tell her Tawny had come from their farm. They had all been in on the secret with Robert.

"I always feel better after being at your place," Amber confided to Dr. Mitchell when the clinic hours were over. "There's such a warmth. I really thought about it and it's because you're like our family was. Too many families today aren't really families, they are just a collection of individuals who happen to live under one roof, each selfishly going his or her own way, not really caring what the others do."

"Yes," the doctor replied seriously. "We enjoy each other." Amber knew that was the key to the Mitchell household. They really appreciated each other, and they were all working together to make their home what they wanted it to be. It wasn't money that cemented them together as a family, it was love and concern.

I want my family to be like that, she thought later that evening as she curled up with Tawny in her lap. Again the thought of Sam Reynolds flashed through her mind. This time she was too tired to push it away. What did it hurt if she dreamed a bit? He would never know. The only one who would be hurt would be herself. Shrugging at the thought, she scattered the coals in the fireplace, carefully fastened the screen, and went to bed. Tomorrow she would go back out to the Kincaids'. Just the thought of that dear new baby was enough to draw her.

A tiny rumble caught her attention. Tawny had crawled out of his basket and had firmly established himself on the foot of her bed. She smiled. How thoughtful Robert was!

She would do everything she could to make him have a happy Thanksgiving. Everything, that is, except love him like he wanted. Even this thought could not keep her awake. Amber slept, the little cat a light weight against her foot.

CHAPTER 7

Thanksgiving morning dawned bright and clear. The snow showers of the past week had ceased, and the world was covered with white. In the pure air you could see for miles. The Seven Devils range in Idaho raised their peaks to the blue sky. It was a day for rejoicing.

Amber was glad the day had come. The clinic work plus her visits to the Kincaid family had kept her extra busy the past week and she was tired. It was good just to have a day off. In spite of the feeling that all was not right with the world in regard to Sam Reynolds, her heart felt at peace for the Harvest service that morning. She was glad for the intercommunity special service held each Thanksgiving morning. Each year the various churches met, taking turns hosting the service of hymns of praise, of thankfulness to God for the harvest. It was a time of rejoicing. Winter loomed ahead with its cold and often harsh realities, but today was a time for thankfulness.

Amber's eyes were bright as she ran up the steps and slipped into the church, choosing a pew near the front and to one side. She had come early, feeling the need for a few moments alone. Bowing her head, she offered a little prayer of her own that she might always do what was right and good, that she might always carry on the work her father had taught her was so important.

Refreshed, she lifted her head as the folks from neighboring communities started to arrive and fill up the church. Robert came in, taking the seat next to her with a smile, and across the room she noticed the Carters. Crystal was pouting a bit — she had planned to sit by Sam Reynolds, who accompanied them, but he had ushered Granny into the pew and seated himself next to her. Granny's eyes twinkled at her spoiled granddaughter's chagrin, but she said nothing.

Sam looked around the church curiously. Amber could see his slight smile from the corner of her eye. She immediately interpreted it as superiority over the simple surroundings. Her blood boiled. How dare this city man come here and make fun of their ways? She remembered the wistfulness in his face when he had first asked why her father had been the man the Chief Editor so admired. Which was the real Sam, the cynic or the seeker? Amber felt torn. Being so attracted to him, yet unwilling to admit it, she noticed every detail, weighing the slightest look in the balance, wondering how or if he could ever fit into her plan of life.

The service was beautiful in its simplicity. Each hymn, illustration, or thought was one of praise and thankfulness. Accustomed to those who sought out the sensational, Sam enjoyed the restfulness of the place. Amber could see his response when several of the farmers and ranchers, Tom Carter included, participated in the service by expressing their gratitude for the homely things of life. Once she caught his direct gaze. He smiled gently, and she returned the look. Without words a healing seemed to come, a mute apology for his actions the night of the Box Social. In that one look was a request for forgiveness, a recognition, and a granting. But in the next moment Sam glanced at Robert, absorbed in the service, and scowled, shattering the moment.

Amber was more shaken than she cared to admit. For one thing, she had attended many Harvest services with her father, and it was strange for him not to be there. Then this business with Sam and with Robert! Closing her eyes for the benediction, she whispered to herself, "Help me trust you for whatever comes."

Comforted, she was able to raise her head and greet the Carters at the door, smiling at Sam and asking how his writing was going. Yes, she would be free Saturday evening if he wanted to come. Yes, she had been thinking of the information he needed about her father. With a vague smile she drifted off, promising to be ready for him at seven Saturday evening.

Sam didn't have long to puzzle over her manner. Crystal had come up, linking her arm in his in the way she had and announcing in a bell-like voice clearly audible throughout the entire group, "Come, Sam, or our turkey will be falling off its bones!"

Amber gave no indication she had heard, but again a strange feeling of loneliness persisted. On the way back to the clinic, to pick up Tawny, she resolutely determined not to let anything about either Sam or Crystal get her down. This was her day, the day her father had taught her to hold in reverence, a special time of year. Her heart lifted. How could anyone be sad or troubled in this beautiful world?

She thought of it again after Robert had picked her up for the short drive to the Kincaids'. They only had time for a short visit, with Robert pronouncing little Amber Lee absolutely perfect and the rest of the family standing around grinning with pleasure at his remarks, but the country lane was a fairyland of white. It was the same at the Mitchells'. They had made sure the road was plowed out of its last snowfall, and the whole family met them on the doorstep.

Dr. Mitchell looked so relaxed in sports shirt and slippers, unlike the busy, efficient doctor who worked with Amber at the clinic. His wife Nell had donned a bright blue dress in honor of the holiday, and her white ruffled apron only added to the pleasant homemaker picture she presented. The five children, ranging in age from two to twelve, had been allowed to change out of their "Sunday best" from the Harvest service, and wore clean but frayed comfortable clothing. Amber's soft green dress brought in the forest tones, and it was a happy group who gathered to the table.

And what a table! The children had proudly decorated it with a homemade brown paper turkey and crayon-colored placemats. The feast was ready, but before eating, Dr. Mitchell held out his hands to those on each side of him, indicating the others were to follow suit.

"Let us give thanks." A mist rose to Amber's eyes as she joined hands with Robert and the smallest Mitchell child.

Dr. Mitchell prayed, "We give thanks for this food and for these friends. We give thanks for thy love and care. We give thanks for the memory of Dr. Mackenzie and what he left us, a pattern of thy service to others. Amen."

"Amen," Robert whispered, eyes full of tenderness for Amber, who could only press his hand gratefully, unable to speak.

"Now can we eat, Dad?" It was the seven-year-old.

"Yes, son." Dr. Mitchell laughed, picking up the big carving knife and attacking the turkey with vigor.

"Not another bite," Amber protested after second helpings on almost everything. The former beautiful table was a shambles.

The children were literally groaning from what they had eaten, and Nell suggested, "Shall we wait and have dessert after the dishes are done?"

There was a chorus of assent. No one felt like mince and apple pies or pumpkin tarts at the moment.

"Come out and build a snowman, Miss

96

Amber," the children invited.

Amber looked at her good dress in dismay. Why hadn't she thought to throw in some older clothes, like Robert had? Already he was in jeans and heavy jacket, ready for a snowball fight. Nell motioned her to the bedroom.

"Help yourself. We're near enough of a size for it to be all right." Amber quickly selected heavy slacks, shoes, and jacket, and was soon out the door, only to be greeted by a flurry of soft snow.

"Why, you," she sputtered, catching up a handful and futilely trying to clean off her face. Catching Robert with his head bent to the ground for more ammunition, she washed his face thoroughly before he could recover from his surprise and straighten up.

There was a gleam in his eyes as he picked her up and tossed her gently in a snowbank, rolling her over and over in the soft snow.

"I give!" Her childish surrender brought them both upright, laughing, two children again, content just to play for a moment, away from the world of life and death they worked in every day.

This is where I belong, Amber thought, but she refused to spoil the day by serious reflection. Besides, how could she be serious with five little Mitchells, Robert, and then even Nell and Dr. Mitchell joining in the fight? Within moments two forts were built and the snowballs were flying thick and fast. It seemed too soon before dusk fell, and it was time for the animals to be cared for. Leaving on her borrowed clothes, Amber happily followed the others to the barn, watched the milking, even helped throw corn to the chickens. Robert had told her on the way out where Tawny had come from, so she was eager to see the mother and other two kittens.

"Mine's the prettiest," she told them all gloatingly, while they laughed at her. Wet snow was streaming from her clothes, her lipstick was a thing of the past. The dampness had only added to her curly hair, and a few locks had escaped from under the stocking cap. She was a mess, yet so filled with enjoyment they all rejoiced. Each of them knew how hard it had been for her to lose her father; it was good to see her so.

"Time for dishes," Nell's quiet voice reminded. There was no protest. The whole troupe swarmed into the kitchen to help. Nell had put the food away earlier, but left the table to play with her family. Now it didn't take long for them to finish up the work and leave the kitchen sparkling clean.

Amber was surprised to find that after all

the exercise she was as ready for pie as the rest of them. Changing back into her green dress, she spoke contentedly to Nell, who was hanging up wet clothes in the laundry room to drip before putting them in the dryer.

"This is how life was meant to be lived, simple, leaving the work to be with one another."

Nell nodded. "It took me a long time to sort out priorities. I wanted everything done just so. Then one day my oldest said, 'Mom, you never have time to do anything with us. Don't you love us?' It really hit me. I reshuffled my attitudes and decided my children and husband were most important. Later when they're grown I will still have the dusting and dishes. Now I want to be with them."

Amber looked toward her hostess warmly. "And you are so many things! No one could ever call you 'just a housewife'! You have made homemaking an art! How many different areas do you cover?"

Nell laughed. "Well, let's see. In addition to wife and mother, there's interior decorator, chef, chauffeur, temporary nurse and veterinarian . . ." She stopped. "I can't really say, Amber! I only know you find time for what you really want to do!" She pointed to the desk where half a dozen beautifully painted Christmas cards were propped up.

"The novelty shop in Wallowa wanted some of these. I did fifteen of each design and they are selling them for me. It keeps my hand in, and the kids are proud as anything. It's been good for them, too; they know I need extra time so they volunteer little 'extras' in addition to keeping their rooms clean and the chores, so 'Mom can paint.' "

"You have a beautiful family," Amber told her sincerely.

"Yes, we do," Nell agreed. "I think living out here away from town has helped. We do things together because we don't have next-door neighbors to rely on."

The evening passed in fun and laughter. Amber felt stuffed again after the delicious homemade pie, and they finished the evening with an old-fashioned sing. Most of the songs were ones the children had known from babyhood and could join in.

"What a dear family!" Amber couldn't help but remark to Robert on their way home, Tawny cuddled close in her lap, his purr a gravelly rumble.

"We could have a home like that," Robert reminded huskily.

The effects of the day were so much that

Amber almost told him she would like nothing better than to establish a home like the Mitchells', but she held back just in time. Not until I'm sure, she told herself. Right now I'm swayed by the warmth, the attraction of the Mitchell way of life. It wouldn't be fair to Robert to say yes, then find out I was wrong. She knew, too, she was being torn by many memories that had included her father, and she would be unfair to make a decision because of loneliness.

If only Sam Reynolds hadn't come to the Wallowa area! But was she being honest? She had been puzzled over what to do about Robert even before the rugged reporter first called.

They were at the Crossroads Clinic before she knew it, and Robert walked her to the door, holding Tawny while she unlocked it.

"Amber," he said, looking directly into her eyes. "You know I want you to love me more than anything else in the world. But I also want you to be true to yourself. Don't worry about things too much. Remember the peace we felt in church this morning? Wait, and see what happens. I love you too much to have you unhappy over me. It hurts more to see you troubled than anything else. Be happy, Amber, and happiness will come to all of us." He bent his dark head and kissed her tenderly. "Good night, Amber, and happy Thanksgiving."

"Happy Thanksgiving, Robert . . . and thank you." The girl's words were choked and she waved as he drove away. Turning slowly, she went into her little home, aware of Tawny's insistent paw reaching up to be petted. Absently she stroked the shining fur, thinking of Robert. She had known what a grand person he was before, but tonight he had, in his own quiet way, advanced his cause more than he could ever know. How understanding! He was too good to her.

Before she prepared for bed she took down an old poetry book she and her father had shared throughout the years. In it was tucked a little verse her father had written when they first built the Crossroads Clinic. It had expressed his feelings. Now as she reread the words she nearly knew by heart they spoke to her as her father would have done.

Two Ways

A traveler came to a crossroads. Two ways met.
One led to fame and fortune . . . and yet
He paused, unable to choose.

The right way, or the left?
What had he to lose?

At last he decided which way his feet
    would trod,
He chose the right way, to happiness . . .
    and God.

"The right way. Which is it?" she asked
Tawny, whose only response was a feline
snore. Robert's words flashed back to her:

"Don't worry. . . . Wait, and see what happens."

He was right. Only time would show her
how to be true to herself and the things she
believed in to the very core of her being.
One thing stood out — no matter where
her path led, it would have to be a path of
service. She was a nurse, dedicated to others. She had chosen it because she felt that
in no other way could she express her
thankfulness for even being alive. It was part
of her, born and bred into her.

". . . the right way, to happiness . . . and
God." She smiled, peace restored. Truly this
had been a day of Thanksgiving.

CHAPTER 8

Saturday night was another crisp, cold evening. Amber had determined not to let her own feelings stand in the way of the story she had promised. Now all she hoped for was the ability to tell it as it had been.

Tawny opened one eye from his sleepy posture on the rug by the hearth, yawned, and dismissed the two humans so intently talking. Why bother with them? It was too warm and comfortable. With a loud meow of indifference, he turned over and went back to sleep.

"Cute little creature." Sam laughed at the lazy little cat. Amber only smiled. He would never know the comfort the little animal had brought her.

"Amber," Sam said, looking directly into her eyes. "I'm glad you didn't tell me your father's story sooner. I've seen what he did here. I've learned to appreciate him for the things he accomplished with the people in this area, to see him through their eyes. I probably couldn't have understood the first chapters of his life if you hadn't made me wait until the last chapters were plain."

"That's why I did it that way," she told him quietly. She was still for a long time, unable to find a thread to start unraveling the long-ago mystery. Then she spoke.

"Much of what I am going to tell you is still highly confidential. For this reason I will leave out some names here and there; the names aren't important anyway." Again she hesitated, then took up the story, a story so strange that Sam forgot to take notes. His pencil lay idle in his lap as she spoke. He began to realize that none of what he had heard or seen had prepared him for the man David Mackenzie had been. He began to admire the doctor with his whole heart, living over the times Amber portrayed. Although she spoke simply there was a world of meaning in her words, all the hopes, fears, joys of the young David Mackenzie, and at last, his disappearance.

When she finished his mind was in a whirl. How could he make a news story from what she had divulged? It could shake Portland Memorial, the very thing Dr. Mackenzie had hoped to avoid! Yet it was the assignment his chief had given him. He was in a quandary. By telling him the story Amber had thrown the burden of what to do with it squarely on his shoulders. Now what could he do?

Suddenly he made his decision. This was too big for him. He turned to Amber.

"If I invite my chief here, would you tell him the story the same way you have told me?" Seeing the doubt creep into her eyes he assured her, "I have already kept him posted on my findings of what your father did in this area. Also, he will come wanting to believe. You needn't be afraid he will misuse the information. Yet I know I can never tell the story the way you have just done." He reflected for a moment.

"I honestly think the chief is less interested in what a good newspaper story there is than in the actual life of your father."

The sincerity in his voice impressed Amber, but she had a further question. "Do you believe what I have told you?"

Her question demanded total honesty and Sam answered carefully, "I understand it. But, Amber, I cannot say that I believe it." Seeing her stricken look he hastened to add, "You grew up with the faith your father had. I know nothing of such feelings. I will promise to consider all you have told me, to have an open mind."

"In other words, you accept the reason my father left Portland Memorial, but you cannot accept the real reason why, or his feeling concerning the Crossroads Calling." Her voice was flat.

"That's it," he admitted, determined to be truthful.

"I suppose it does sound incredible in today's world," she whispered, her eyes misty with memory. "Do you think your chief will be able to . . . ?"

Sam finished her broken sentence. "Much more than I can accept. He longs for something to believe in. Besides, he knew and loved your father. That's why I want him to come."

Amber nodded assent. Somehow she must make these men know what her father had done was real, not a quixotic gesture. When Sam had gone, after promising to let her know when Don Baker would arrive, she felt a bit forlorn. Going to the big picture of her father and mother she murmured, "You said it would be almost unbelievable. But why is it so hard for people to accept simple things?" She remembered asking her father the same question several years ago.

"It is always easy to believe in what you see," he had replied. Troubled, she turned away, wondering what Sam's chief would think.

It was a whole week before she saw Sam again, a week filled with patients and trips into remote areas. The Kincaids really didn't need any more home visits but she found herself dropping in on her way back from other calls. Their little family was so glad to see her she just couldn't stay away.

Shortly after the clinic closed on Saturday, Sam and the chief arrived. Again the cosy little home stretched out arms of welcome. Don Baker gave a sigh of pure contentment as he settled into a worn but comfortable chair by the fire, cuddling Tawny into his lap, and prepared to listen. In spite of his beautiful Portland mansion, there was something in this little cottage that evaded his more beautiful house. This was a home, not a house, he amended. He could understand how Sam had been so taken with the girl. Amber was lovely in a soft gold pants outfit, the firelight playing on her delicate features.

Her heart beat faster as she prepared to tell her father's story for the second time. If there was any way she could put into words what her father had actually been! Forcing herself to a more quiet attitude, she inquired about Don Baker's trip. It had been a grand day for his flight to LaGrande from Portland and he had thoroughly enjoyed it.

At last he set aside the cup, drained of every drop of hot chocolate, and said, "And now, my dear, tell me of your father . . . and my friend." There was something in his voice that had the effect of breaking up the dam in her heart that had been there since her father's death. Sam was amazed. The story she told was the same one he had heard, but told in the light of the editor's expectant trust, it sounded completely different.

David Mackenzie had wanted to be a minister, not a doctor. From the time he was a small boy his dream was to become a minister and be sent into the field to battle against sin and ignorance. Taken from his plans by the war, he became a chaplain's assistant. The man he worked with was an outstanding person. No creed or denomination stood in the way of his loving ministry. From him David learned that the first requirement for ministry was not desire, but love. Together they went to the front, assisting where they could, helping where they were able. Many times David learned to look down on young men whose life blood was ebbing away, comforting as best he could. Many times he felt powerless to stop the tide of hatred that produces war, or to care for those he ministered to.

In the last big battle before being wounded and shipped home he came across a strange sight. A crooked signpost, one arm leaning toward the left, one toward the right, had survived the holocaust. At the foot of it lay David's chaplain. He had been badly hurt, yet he recognized it was David who had come for him.

"Medic, medic!" the frantic young man called, but all of the staff were too far away to hear him. Using what limited knowledge he had, David helped his beloved superior the best he knew how, but it wasn't enough — his chaplain died. He died gloriously, with a smile on his face, pointing to the signpost at the crossroads, the one leading to the right.

Amber's voice broke, and for a moment they didn't think she could continue but, steadying her voice, she took up the story.

When the rest of the outfit came they found David with his chaplain in his arms, crying like a baby, bitterly wailing that he hadn't been able to help more. But in those moments a determination was born. There was more than one way to serve God. He was going to go to medical school after his own wounds healed. He would make God his partner in everything he did for humanity, just as he would have done in the clerical field. He would fight the war of poverty, of sickness, of useless death. He would become like Lucas, the Great Physician. Never had anyone studied harder than David Mackenzie, and he graduated with great honors. Yet his voice was broken, his eyes wet as he took the Hippocratic pledge to spend his life in the service of mankind . . . and of his God.

David had learned to know another God while he was on the battlefield, not the one so many people find on Sunday, keep on the shelf during the rest of the week, but a living, guiding Presence who walked with him. He learned to never prepare for surgery or make a diagnosis without a quick prayer that he might be an instrument of healing in those eternal hands. Because of it, he rose to heights of fame in Portland. He became a sought-after surgeon, and finally, Chief of Staff at the Portland Memorial Hospital.

Amber paused again, and the editor leaned forward in his chair. It was coming, the story he had wanted to hear for so many years. Gripping the arms of the chair, he listened to the most amazing test David Mackenzie's faith had ever known, the challenge to keep the Golden Rule of "doing unto others" he had believed in so long.

Against the warning of some of the advisory board, Dr. Mackenzie had added to his staff a new man from out of state. Although young, the doctor was brilliant, and David saw in him the promise of an outstanding surgeon. He knew the new doctor had a history of wildness at times, yet he was willing to give the man a chance to prove himself.

"My father always believed and looked for the best in people," Amber told them quietly.

Through the following weeks the Chief of Staff did have faith in the new doctor, who seemed to be proving himself. Then one night it happened. The early-morning screams of the ambulance brought in three patients from a nearby burning building. It was necessary to call for extra help. The new doctor was located in a nearby bar. He was off duty, but told Dr. Mackenzie he would be all right. Hurrying home, he showered and changed, trying to remove all evidence of his heavy drinking.

Dr. Mackenzie only saw the doctor at a distance when he reported for duty, and he was too busy to do more than wave in the direction of the room where the third patient lay awaiting attention. When he finished his own work he stepped to the doorway of the room. Horrified, he saw the young doctor asleep in a chair next to the bed. The burn victim was dead. He woke up the young doctor and hustled him out a back way, then hastened to the room. Checking the man's chart, he saw there would only have been one chance in a thousand that the patient could have made it through even with the finest attention . . . but he had been denied that attention.

The next day Dr. Mackenzie went to the young doctor and placed it before him, the terrible thing he had done.

"I realize the man wouldn't have lived anyway," he told him gravely. "But your condition and your responsibility is inexcusable."

The younger man pleaded bitterly. He had learned his lesson. He was not an alcoholic, only took a social drink to relax, but never again would he touch a drop. The fact he could have killed someone in his carelessness was shock enough to last a lifetime.

"Give me another chance," he begged, tears in his eyes. "I promise before you and God to become the kind of doctor I should be, the kind that every doctor should be."

Dr. Mackenzie stood at a different kind of crossroads now — he must be judge and jury. After a long moment he said, "I think you will." He promised to take care of the matter. No one would ever know what the young doctor had failed to do.

Amber went on to tell how the Chief of Staff had met with the Board of Directors. He told them a patient had died and it had been his fault. In his own way of thinking, he had been responsible, as he felt personally responsible for every employee or patient in his hospital. Over their strong protest, not knowing the full circumstances, he resigned. Not one of the Board of Directors could see why. Dr. Mackenzie had sacrificed himself, his excellent position, his eminence, for the sake of a less worthy human being, but it was part of his creed. He took his family and wandered for a while, looking for a place where he could be useful. There was no cloud on his medical record, only in his own mind. Any hospital would welcome him. But now that he was away from the city, he suddenly felt tired. All those years, the war, his training, he needed rest. "I remember when we first saw this country." Amber's eyes were tranquil, remembering happy ties that bound her to her family.

"Dad brought Mom and me into the area for a trip. We were impressed with the simple way of life and Dad told us sometime we were going to come back and live here. We laughed at the time — we were established elsewhere. But he loved this place, and soon after that trip he said he had come to a crossroads in his life again. Which way?" She slowly drew out the little poem Dr. Mackenzie had written.

"A traveler came to a crossroads. Two
    ways met.
One led to fame and fortune . . . and yet
He paused, unable to choose.

The right way, or the left?
What had he to lose?

At last he decided which way his feet
    would trod,
He chose the right way, to happiness . . .
    and God."

Amber's story was finished. It was very still in the room, the silence broken only by the editor's involuntary catching his breath and blowing his nose hard. Almost timidly he asked, "Then your father's Crossroads Calling was based on religion?"

Amber took a long time to answer. "Not religion as we call it so often. His Crossroads Calling was a way of life. And in it he did

115

find happiness . . . and God."

"I'd give everything I possess to have your faith — and his," Don Baker blurted out.

Amber smiled gently at the successful man, now groping for something to believe in.

"It's all there for the asking. My father was no plaster saint, he was a flesh and blood man. But he was a man with vision. He saw that the only way to find peace or happiness in today's world was to have something to believe in. The former idols of past generations had not kept the world from war, or hatred, or despair. He wanted a way of life for right now. If he couldn't change the entire world, then he would change his own world, and perhaps the world he touched with the medical skill and knowledge he felt was a gift as well as an acquired and learned thing. He did change his world. He changed what could have been bitterness to life and hope. Listen!"

She leaned forward, a glowing figure. "Never did my father expect to be rewarded for what he did, for what he was. Yet he was rewarded beyond what any man could ask. I could name the man whose place he took when he resigned. You would recognize him immediately as a leading authority today in the world of medicine. What greater joy than knowing my father had made that possible? There are other stories —" She glanced at Sam. "Some of the people Sam has told you about, others you can meet if you stay long enough. These people were just as important to my father as the man who later became famous! He taught me that every human soul is of equal worth, not in our eyes, but in the whole plan of creation. It is just as necessary to minister to the lowly as the great. That's why I am here now. I believe, as Dad taught, that our greatest reward comes in what we can do for others."

A strange lump formed in Sam's throat as she spoke. His fears on the day he had decided to write a book swept over him. This was Amber's world, but was it his own, even though he loved its beauty?

His feeling was reflected in the chief's question to Amber.

"How could someone such as I find that faith, that determination to live for others, and where would I go?"

Amber weighed her words carefully. "I cannot tell you that, Mr. Baker. When you come to your crossroads you will know. And it will have to be your own decision which way is the right way for you. No human being can choose for another. That's why my father never once influenced me in my choice of career, or of where I would work. He knew I could never be happy following his Crossroads Calling; it had to be my own . . . and it is."

The older man stood. Taking both her hands in his own, he said huskily, "Amber, you will never know what your story has meant to me. Maybe someday I will be able to tell you, or show you. Think of me sometimes, will you?"

Amber's heart warmed toward the lonely man before her and she said impulsively, "Don't stay away too long, Mr. Baker. Come back. Come when spring covers the hillsides, or when summer heat shimmers in the valley. Come when autumn turns the world to gold, but come."

"I will," he promised, and a spark lit his eyes that had not been there before. "Need another newspaper around here?"

Amber chose to take his joking remark seriously. "Yes, sir. We can always use another good newspaper here."

When they had gone Amber sat in front of the flames for a long time, Tawny in her lap. She felt drained. The story had taken a lot from her, she realized now. What would the two men do with it? They had both promised not to use anything that would harm either the memory of Dr. Mackenzie or his protege, and she knew they would keep that promise. Sam had confessed he was going to stay and try a book, and had obtained the whole-hearted approval of his chief. After all, his assignment was over now.

Amber remembered the look on each face as she told her story. Her heart fell a bit. She knew the chief had been much more receptive to Dr. Mackenzie's way of life than Sam had. It was hard for him, hard-working, full of drive that he was, to imagine anyone giving up his career for the sake of another man who might or might not turn out to be worthy of the gift. Yet she knew he had been thinking about her story since he had first heard it a week before. There had been an added tolerance.

Could their lives ever match enough to be fused into the kind of relationship Amber wanted in marriage? Although attracted to him, Amber really wondered about it. Robert's face flashed to mind, and a feeling of warmth spread over her. Why couldn't she just have fallen in love with him? But then, things were never that easy. Her father taught her the joy of living came from the daily decisions that demanded attention.

As Amber turned off her bedlamp a little later she offered a quick prayer for the two men who had been in her home that night.

Each seemed to need peace. Each seemed to be struggling in an attempt to find happiness and meaning in life. Had they been sent to the Crossroads Clinic for a reason? She knew their coming would affect her life but didn't quite know how . . . not yet. The white curtain fluttered at the window as a little breeze rattled the glass. Tawny gave a meow of protest, then settled down to undisturbed slumber. But the daughter of David Mackenzie lay sleepless, filled with a strange peace and joy that she had been able to share her beloved father's story with the two men who had come to her home that evening. And her last words of prayer were thankfulness that she had known such a wonderful father.

CHAPTER 9

An unfamiliar sound roused Amber from her deep sleep. Had she been dreaming? No, there it was again. Never one to be afraid, still that strange sound sent a chill through her. She knew she wouldn't be able to sleep until she checked it out. Hastily wrapping a warm robe around her, she listened again.

It came from the direction of the clinic. Yet everything there was locked up. Her illuminated clock showed three o'clock. There was no reason for anyone to be in the clinic then. If an emergency arose, the caller would have rung the night bell that connected with her living quarters.

Cautiously Amber stole into the clinic. The sound, like scraping, seemed to come from the nurse's station area. Snapping the wall switch, she flooded the room with light. There by the drug cabinet, like a wounded animal at bay, stood a long-haired boy. He clutched something in his hands. One arm hung limply at his side. Too startled to think clearly for a moment, Amber and the intruder stared at one another, then her nurse's training asserted itself.

"You're hurt!" In one quick motion she was at the teenager's side. Ignoring his protest, she grasped the limp arm and found a pressure point. The boy thrust his other hand in his jacket and attempted to jerk away.

"Stand still," she commanded, and there was something in her voice that kept him in place. She could see the suffering in his eyes, the painful flinch as she led him to the desk. Asking no questions, she expertly dressed the wound, then motioned him into a chair. All at once the stiffening seemed to leave the stubborn spine, and the boy collapsed into the chair, a groan escaping his tightly clenched lips.

Compassion filled Amber's gaze at the bent head. How old was he? Fourteen? Sixteen? She had never seen him before. From the looks of him he had traveled quite a way. There was mud on his boots and melted snow on his worn blue jeans. He looked like he hadn't had anything to eat for several days.

Without hesitation she made her decision.

"Come back here," she ordered, leading him to her living quarters. After poking up the fire and turning the thermostat higher, she forced him to the couch and covered him with a blanket. It only took minutes to warm soup and make toast and hot chocolate to go with it. At first the boy refused to eat, but gradually the warmth of the room stilled him and he finished every bite. Not until the food was gone did Amber ask, "Why were you in the drug cabinet?" She hesitated for only a moment, then added crisply, "Are you an addict?"

Sheer disgust filled the boy's eyes. "No!" In spite of his ragged appearance, the boy's spontaneous reply convinced Amber. He hung his head, then looked her straight in the eye.

"I fell and hurt my arm. It got so bad I didn't know what to do. When I saw the sign Crossroads Clinic I knew there would be something to ease the pain." Sheepishly he pulled his right hand from his pocket. Wadded in it was a great roll of cotton and a bottle of aspirin!

It took every ounce of self-discipline for Amber to control the involuntary wave of laughter that threatened to escape. She could see there was a pride in this strange boy. It would never do to laugh. Instead she said sternly, "Why didn't you ring the bell? How did you get in, anyway?"

"I hated to bother you. The window was open a little bit, so I slipped through. I hit my arm on the sill; I guess that's why it started to bleed again."

Amber shook her head reprovingly, but said nothing. This was not the time for lectures. She only had one more question.

"Who are you?"

For a moment she didn't think he was going to answer, then almost reluctantly he said, "I'm Charlie Vickers."

Only Amber's rigorous training kept her from staring at him open-mouthed. Instead she merely nodded and told him, "All right, Charlie. You're to stay here tonight."

Over his protest she fixed him a comfortable bed on the couch. Almost before she finished making it and putting the kitchen to rights the boy was asleep, his face white with the strain he had been under.

Amber found sleep had gone for her. There was too much to think about. Charlie Vickers, foster son of old Vagabond Vic, the most notorious ne'er-do-well in the valley! She sighed. What chance did he have? Was there anything she could do? A thousand questions crowded her mind. Why had he been out so late? It was twenty miles to his shack. Had he really fallen, or . . . ? She had heard Vagabond treated him meanly, but nothing had ever been proved. Determinedly she made up her mind. Tomorrow she would find out just what was going on! It was Sunday, and she was free. If that boy was being mistreated she would personally contact the authorities. For all the wonderful foster homes there were, once in a blue moon someone like Vagabond Vic came along. He had put up a good front and taken the boy to live with him, but if the busy office hadn't been checking recently, it could be an entirely different story.

At last she fell into a troubled sleep, waking to a feeling of something wrong. The morning light brought it all back — she had overslept. Amber had planned to be up before Charlie awoke, but when she ran to the living room, only a neatly folded pile of blankcts mct her gaze. Frantically looking around the room, she noticed a note on the battered desk.

Thanks for the patch job. I took the cotton and aspirin.

Charlie

Tears of frustration stung her eyelids. Why had she overslept, this morning of all mornings! She paced the floor until Tawny's plaintive meow recalled her to the present. After feeding the cat, she dressed and stepped to the clinic door. Maybe Charlie hadn't been gone long. Perhaps if she got out the jeep she could find him . . . but which way would he have gone?

She brushed the tears away, threw on the first clothes she could find in the closet, and started out, thinking rapidly. Vagabond lived north, so the boy wouldn't have gone in that direction if he was really running away, and she had a feeling he was. There was nothing much to the east or west for many miles and he would be smart enough to realize that in his condition he couldn't go far. She watched carefully as she headed south along the snowy road. Every moving creature or tree shadow came in for close observation, and about three miles down the road her diligence was rewarded. Charlie had stopped to rest against a fence.

"Time for breakfast," she told him quietly. He was too all in to even register the slightest protest, and as she started to turn she saw red at his fingertips. The wound was bleeding again. Compressing her lips tightly, she continued south instead of heading back to the clinic. At first he didn't notice. He seemed slightly dazed. But when he opened his eyes he was immediately on the alert.

"Where are you taking me?" he demanded hoarsely, fear filling his eyes. Her quiet voice seemed to reassure him.

"To Dr. Meacham. That cut evidently needs stitches in order to heal properly." For a moment he looked as if he might be planning to open the door and jump but she kept her tones even.

"Dr. Meacham is a wonderful doctor. He can fix your arm as good as new." She went on to tell him amusing anecdotes of some of Robert's work and succeeded in getting a half smile from him once or twice. When they arrived at Robert's home, she was relieved to see his car in the driveway. Evidently he hadn't left for church yet.

With a keen glance at Charlie she told him, "You may as well come right in. Dr. Meacham keeps all necessary emergency equipment for such routine cuts in his doctor's bag. He won't have to go to the office." She blessed Robert's understanding in not asking any questions until he had taken care of the arm. After injecting a local anesthetic, she deftly helped swab the angry-looking area before the doctor took stitches. Charlie's face was set as he watched them, but he made no sound. They finished with a dusting of antibiotic powder and a clean bandage, held in place with a heavier pad.

"Now," Dr. Meacham asked, "what's this all about?"

In simple words Amber told him what had happened the night before. Shooting Amber an unexplainable glance, Dr. Meacham asked Charlie pointblank, "Just where do you think you're going?"

"Anywhere!" The word burst from the boy's lips before he could hold it back, then he fell into silence. Perhaps his single exclamation told Robert and Amber more than anything else could have done. Instead of discussing it in front of Charlie, the doctor called his housekeeper and asked her to take the boy upstairs to a room. They lived in a two-story house that had been owned by Robert's parents and grandparents.

"That arm is nothing to fool around with," he told the startled Charlie. "I want to keep you here the rest of today and tonight to be sure no infection has set in. It was pretty dirty."

After the first shock, Charlie seemed to accept his words at face value and meekly followed the housekeeper.

Robert turned to Amber. "Someone has hurt that boy worse than the wound on his arm." His face became stern. "I'm going to find out about it."

He ignored Amber's comment of, "But it's Sunday. You can't get anyone now!" and dialed the telephone.

"Judge Parker? I've got a young boy here, Charlie Vickers. You know, Vagabond Vic's son. He's been hurt and I want to keep him. What's the best thing to do? Also, I strongly suspect Vic's been mistreating the kid. He's probably fifteen or so." He paused to listen for a moment. "Yes, I'll drive out and tell Vic where he is. Maybe I can learn something about why the boy left. Thanks, Judge."

Putting down the phone, he smiled at Amber. "Want to take a ride this afternoon?" He didn't need her warm smile for assent. She would take her car back and he would pick her up a little later. It was getting too late for church, so as soon as Robert could have a little talk with Charlie they would go out to Vic's.

It was a beautiful drive. Heavy snow was hanging from the limbs of the evergreen trees, while bare branches were encased in icy sheathes, glistening in the sun. Amber lifted her face to the sparkling air. She was unwilling to probe her feelings at the moment. When there was time she would take out the new sensations she felt at the precise way Robert had gone to the heart of the problem. She had been so used to him as an old friend it seemed there were no other facets to his personality, but now he loomed different. She hadn't known he could look so grim and unyielding as when he picked her up for the trip to Vagabond Vic's.

"He has been mistreated," he told her shortly and would say no more. Something in his attitude kept Amber from questioning him. To distract him a bit from the unpleasantness she felt sure lay ahead, several times Amber called his attention to a particularly beautiful spot, but his usual response to the country they both loved was missing. At last she too lapsed into silence, broken only by the swish of tires on the snowy road.

The last few miles in to Vic's place was pretty rugged. It took all the strength of the jeep to make it. It was a good thing they hadn't tried to bring Robert's car — it wouldn't have got beyond the paved highway. At last they pulled up in front of the dismal building Charlie called home.

Robert looked anxiously at Amber. "Maybe you'd better stay in the car."

She shook her head obstinately. "No. You may need a witness to what happens." Reluctantly he agreed, seeing the wisdom of her remark. At first there was no answer to their vigorous knocks on the worn door, but at last it opened a crack.

"You folks want something?" The question was more like a snarl, and two small, beady eyes glared hate at them from under a tangled thatch of hair.

"It's about Charlie."

A string of profanity followed, until Robert said, "Stop! That's enough of that! I know exactly why that boy left here and what you've done. Watch that language!"

The door grudgingly opened a trifle further, just enough to show the dim interior of the filthy shack.

"You better get that boy back here or I'll have the law on ye!"

Robert laughed outright. "The law! You're a fine one to talk about the law! And as for Charlie" — he stopped and looked full in the evil old face — "he won't be back. I am personally asking for a hearing by the foster-child association. You'll never have anyone here again to mistreat."

"Get out! Get out, both of ye!" The sheer force of his hissing breath drove Amber back a step. She felt something so terribly evil here. This old man, this lonely spot. If he wanted to hurt them who would know? Clutching Robert's arm she whispered, "Please, let's go."

Robert hesitated, unwilling to back down from the challenge offered, but after a glance into Amber's pale face he conceded.

"You'll be called for the hearing," he shot back at the closing door, but only a wicked sneer on the rapidly disappearing face answered him.

As they got into the car the old man once more came to the door, this time opening it wide, holding a vicious brute of a dog by the collar.

"Next time you come out here I'll sick Satan on ye," he called. The dog, straining at the leash, saliva dripping from the open mouth, indeed looked like Satan himself.

"Robert, quick," Amber called desperately as the dog tore loose from the cackling old man, reaching the car just as Robert slammed the door on those hungry jaws.

Robert was pale as they drove away. "I hadn't meant to tell you, Amber, but I want you to remember that dog. Now remember the wounded arm Charlie is carrying."

In horror she looked at him. "You don't mean . . ." Disbelief choked off the rest of the sentence.

"Yes. If I hadn't believed Charlie's story, I would now. That arm was torn open by a dog, not a fall in some ditch. We may be required to testify."

Amber still couldn't believe it. "But why?"

"Vic probably starves the dog. He wouldn't want Charlie to leave, it would cut his income. Charlie told me he tried once before and then couldn't make it past Satan. Yesterday when he did get away Vagabond Vic missed him and went looking for him in his old truck. Charlie didn't think he set the dog on him on purpose, just as today that beast pulled away. He couldn't hold him. Before Charlie could get him with the stick he carried Satan had ripped his arm. Then Charlie got in one good hit and knocked the dog down.

"Strangely enough, the only thing Vic really cares about is that ugly dog. Enraged, still he couldn't bypass the dog lying there dazed. While he stopped to see about Satan Charlie ran for all he was worth, making it to the highway. A passing neighbor gave him a ride, thinking he was hitchhiking to some school activity. Charlie didn't let on he was hurt, just wrapped his shirtsleeve around his arm and got off near the clinic. He said he must have passed out for a little while because when he came to it was dark. He walked for what seemed like hours, must have been in circles, until he saw the Crossroads Clinic sign. You know the rest."

Amber's heart burned inside. How could

133

anyone live like that? She whispered a little prayer that Charlie had come to the clinic. Her eyes popped open at a sudden thought, "So that's why you gave Charlie a tetanus shot!"

He nodded, his face set. "Yes, and after I talked with him I told the housekeeper to keep a close watch on him. If there's any sign of fever whatsoever we'll start rabies shots, just in case. However, for all Satan's fierceness, I didn't see any sign that he was rabid, just mean."

Amber shivered. It was hard to believe the events of the last few hours, and she had a sinking feeling they hadn't heard the last of Vic.

CHAPTER 10

As Robert had predicted, Amber was called on to testify at the investigation of Vagabond Vic's treatment of Charlie. She told the story clearly, how the boy had awakened her in order to get help for his badly hurt arm, how she and Robert had visited Vic, and the ensuing scene.

It didn't take the board long to rule against the wicked old man, whose malevolent gaze had never left Amber's and Robert's faces during the entire proceeding. As he brushed past them on his way out, his evil stare was full of hatred and Amber heard him mutter, ". . . get even!" With a last piercing look he was gone, leaving her strangely uneasy. Amber had never feared many things in life but this man was so evil, so vengeful, that now she feared what he might do.

The remaining days before Christmas kept her so busy she had little time to think of the old man. The cold and flu season had struck viciously. The clinic was packed, and many times she was called into the surrounding area for home visits. One of them took her back to the Carters. It had been some time since she had seen them or Sam Reynolds, now firmly entrenched in Granny's cabin for the winter. She found her heart beating rapidly as she approached the Carter home, but Sam wasn't there. A pang of relief mixed with disappointment filled her. Although she longed to see him, there was still a question as to how he had taken her father's story. She knew he needed time to think over the crossroads calling way of life that she and Robert had grown up with. She was fair enough to see that to a stranger, raised without much idea of faith, it sounded farfetched. Still she hoped wistfully that he would be able to accept her father as he had really been.

Amber was struck with the change in Crystal Carter. While her blonde beauty remained the same, gone were the flirtatious ways that had been so much a part of her. They had been replaced with a new sweetness, a sincerity Amber had never noticed in the girl.

"Would you like to stop by and see Sam?" she asked Amber a bit hesitantly.

"Yes, do," Granny croaked from her bed where a touch of the flu had kept her for the past few days. "That boy needs checking on."

Amber's heart leaped and she answered shyly, "Why, yes, Crystal."

Crystal smiled. "Mom has some things she wants taken up. Let's see if Billy wants to go with us."

Amber was amazed at the genuine love and concern Crystal showed Billy as she asked him to go, receiving a warwhoop of delight from that young man. Seeing her surprise, Crystal told her, "Billy and I have been getting reacquainted the past few weeks. It's been glorious outdoor weather so we've been sledding and snowshoeing nearly every day we could be spared from home. Sam has been with us a lot, too."

Amber looked at the girl quickly to see if there was any of the former smugness in her tone, but only contentment and joy showed in the glowing face above her red ski outfit. So that's it, Amber thought, enlightened. After all the masculine attention Crystal has received all her life, at last she's fallen in love. The thought made her stop, look, and listen to her own feelings, but there was no time for introspection — they had arrived at Sam's temporary home.

"Crystal! Amber! Billy!" The surprise and pleasure in Sam's tone was the same for each of them. Joyously he led them inside.

"Guess I must have known someone was coming today. I even swept the floor!" Amber laughed at his statement. Granny's cabin was as spotless as ever.

"You mean you really keep it this clean?" she challenged.

Sam shot a warm glance at Crystal. "Oh, I get help." Again Amber experienced a strange sinking of heart. There was such a comradeship in his tone as he smiled at the tiny blonde girl who looked up at him, heart in eyes. What chance had she, Amber, against such a doll-like creature? To cover up her confusion she demanded he tell her everything he had been doing, from chores to writing.

The following hour was happy for them all. Sam leaned back and relaxed, Billy chased the dog in the fields outside until cold and rosy, then came back to curl up in front of the fire. Amber and Crystal listened breathlessly to Sam's partly written book. He had protested when they insisted he share with them what he had done so far.

"It's only in rough form. You won't like it." When they continued to plead he had given in and rather diffidently started reading. As he got deeper into the story he lost his diffidence and read with all the feeling he possessed. It was good, very good. Even the two girls, used to the country he described, felt they were seeing their homeland through new eyes.

"I have chosen the title," he told them quietly, with a special look for Amber. "It is to be 'Two Ways for the Traveler.' " Amber's eyes filled with tears, remembering her father's poem. What a tribute! Did it mean he was learning the secret of the crossroads calling?

As the evening wore on, Sam proudly prepared a snack, showing off his cooking skill with potatoes roasted in the fire, bacon fried to a turn, and a salad composed of "every vegetable available," as he put it. Once he laughed and told them something rather sheepishly about his book.

"I have been fascinated with the word Lostine. To me it must be an Indian word, mysterious, full of meaning. I determined to find out what it was and weave it into my story. Every chance I got I went to some of the little towns around, sought out the old-timers and asked its meaning, but no one seemed to know. Even Granny Carter, who has lived here all her life, didn't know, but she suggested I go to the newspaper office.

They would be sure to have something on it." He stopped to laugh loudly at his own expense.

"I wish I had never gone! After all my mental buildup, they found a book for me that told about the early days and how the towns were named. I found that Wallowa means 'Land of the Winding Waters,' which I thought was beautiful, but still Lostine was my target. What a letdown! It was named by an early settler after his hometown of Lostine, Kansas! There went all my romantic dreams of finding a beautiful, hidden meaning!"

The girls laughed until they cried.

"You could write to Lostine, Kansas," Amber told him. Sam shook his head.

"Nope. I'm going to go back to my original feeling that Lostine has some beautiful meaning! If I write, I'll probably find out it's some family name or something. In this case, ignorance is bliss!"

At last it was time to go. Sam waved goodbye as Amber turned the jeep. Billy was busy with his own thoughts and hopped out as soon as they reached the Carter place, but Crystal sat still for a moment.

"Amber, I want to tell you something." Her voice was low, but the words clear. "For what it may be worth, I'm in love with

Sam." Her voice was even. "I know he thinks the world of you, and it may never make any difference to him, or he may never know how I feel. I'm not asking anything, either, but I felt I wanted you to know." She was quiet for a long time, gazing out at the snow-covered scene before them.

"Ever since I can remember I've been envious of you. That's why I made it a point to cut you down whenever I could, especially in front of the different guys. Oh, I know, there were a lot of them after me, but it wasn't the same. I was someone they admired, someone to take places and show off. But with you it wasn't like that. I've never seen a man yet that didn't get that 'little white home with a picket fence' look in his eyes when he watched you. Although you're a wonderful nurse, men see you as a wife and mother, too. That's the way it should be.

"It took a long time to realize how jealous I was. I wanted people to admire and love me the way they did you. Then Sam came. At first he was a new man in town, another to conquer. Then I got to know him. He treated me differently, with respect, as a real person and not just someone for a casual date to show off in front of the other guys. I began to see the difference. It really taught me something. I don't have to just be 'Miss Popularity' . . . I want a home, and kids, and to be idolized by my husband. I know I can have it, too. Probably not with Sam, but sometime, with someone."

Amber's heart turned toward the girl, so open in her feelings.

"I'm sure you will," she said quietly. "Crystal, does it make any difference to you that Sam is from Portland? Although he loves this country, he may not want to stay forever. Portland offers him a challenge — he may even get to be Chief Editor of the *Star* there. Would it bother you to leave here?"

Crystal looked at her in surprise. "Why, no, Amber. When you love someone, place doesn't matter. All that matters is being with him."

Amber was silenced. She knew in her heart that although she too was attracted to Sam, it would make a vast chasm between them if he chose to return to the city. Her work was here, her life.

Crystal seemed to read her thoughts. "I'm different than you, Amber. While I admire a woman who can successfully combine a career with marriage, my career will be marriage. Besides, I'm a good typist. If things ever did work out with Sam, and he continues to write, he will have a built-in secretary!" She giggled, lightening the serious moment.

"I'm not going to tell him that. It might be the deciding factor!" Amber joined in the laugh, but her mind was whirling. She knew she had a lot of serious thinking to do.

"Crystal, thank you for sharing these things with me. I know it hasn't been easy, but I appreciate your doing so. I feel I should be equally honest. I do like Sam, but I don't know if I love him or not. His decision about here or Portland would make a great difference. Then too, there's Robert. I know I love him, but I'm not just sure exactly how, whether it's the way I should feel for marriage."

The smaller girl's eyes grew old and wise. "Amber, when you are in love, the way you want to be, you'll know it. You'll be willing to sacrifice a lot if it takes that." Her tone was serious, and Amber realized more than ever how the girl had changed from a frivolous flirt to a mature woman in the past month or so. Reaching a mittened hand across to her, Amber smiled again.

"Crystal, I hope things work out the way that will bring the most happiness . . . to all of us."

She was startled by Crystal's confident answer. "Of course they will, Amber."

Curious, she asked, "How can you be so sure?"

The other girl thought for a moment then gazed her full in the eyes. "Sam told me of your father, of his feeling about the Cross-roads Calling. I believe every word of it. If a person chooses the right way, it will lead them to happiness . . . and to God."

"Oh, Crystal!" Amber's tears spilled over. She didn't tell her that it was a shock to find Crystal could so readily believe. She wouldn't have suspected the necessary depths in this girl, in spite of her sturdy heritage of God-fearing people, to under-stand and accept David Mackenzie's motto.

Crystal went on. "Sam will believe it, too." There was a ring of truth in her voice. "We have discussed it for hours, when he comes down to visit, or when Billy and I take sup-plies up. Right now he is like a ship with a broken oar, frantically paddling with the one remaining shred of reason. But the time will come when he will reach out for something more than the frail security he now holds."

"Frail security." Amber repeated the words. She could understand now Crystal's deep feeling for Sam. In all honesty she had to admit she had no such feeling within herself for the rugged visitor. She also saw Crystal as a new person, and was glad.

"I thought I loved your father when he came to take care of us, but I realize now I only knew him as a doctor, not a man," Crystal said. "Now I can appreciate all he really was." Throwing off her mood of seriousness, she clambered out of the jeep.

"And I love his daughter, too, now that I'm not jealous any more!" Giving Amber no chance to reply, she made a gamine face and ran lightly up the front steps, leaving Amber to follow her with her eyes, a new feeling of friendship for the tiny blonde.

Amber welcomed the long drive home. It gave her a chance to sort out some of her own feelings. Crystal had really hit the nail on the head with some of her remarks, which now came back to break into her solitary thoughts.

Later that night she sat across a small table from Robert in the same steak house in LaGrande that Sam had taken her a few weeks before. In her whirling world of appraisal, Robert was a dear and familiar figure. Yet was he? She remembered the feeling she had had when he dealt with Charlie and Vagabond Vic. She remembered the feeling that in many ways this good friend was a stranger to her. Tonight, after her talk with Crystal, she looked at him closely, scrutinizing the smallest motion, weighing each word, until at last he laughingly asked her, "Amber, what's wrong with you? Those big yellow eyes are looking at me as though you had never seen me before!"

Her answer was slow in coming and when it did, it made his heart beat high with an upsurge of hope.

"Perhaps I never really have, Robert. Perhaps I never really have."

Wise enough not to demand an explanation he only eyed her steadily, noting the flush on her beautiful face.

"What did you do with yourself today?" he asked, feeling it might be just as well to change the subject.

Eagerly she bent forward, leaving her steak to cool on the plate. Never had she looked more beautiful than in the soft yellow gown she wore so often. Her face lighted up as she told him, "Crystal and Billy and I went out to see Sam."

Her words hit him full force like ice water in the spring runoff.

"I see." He cut his meat steadily, controlling the sinking in his heart. So that's why she was so radiant, she had seen Sam. Determined not to let her notice anything amiss, he questioned, "How's everything out there?"

"Oh, fine!" She was off on a river of words, telling of how they spent the afternoon, overlooking in her eagerness the fact that Robert had grown quieter and quieter, methodically finishing the excellent dinner that tasted like sawdust.

She finished with, "And Crystal! Oh, Robert, have you seen the change in Crystal?"

This was safer ground for him and he could agree wholeheartedly.

"Yes, I have. You know, I went out a couple times to see if the Carters wouldn't mind taking Charlie Vickers until it's decided what to do with him. She's really a knockout! I never did like her too well when she was trying to capture every man in sight, but now . . ." His approval was a little pool of silence between them.

Now it was Amber's turn for a sinking heart. Robert had given full expression to what she had seen in Crystal, but perversely, she wished he hadn't! What's wrong with me? she asked herself impatiently. Am I turning out like Crystal used to be . . . wanting every man around for myself? Her face flamed scarlet at the thought and she dropped her fork, managing a feeble smile at her escort.

"I think I must be extra tired." Immedi-

147

ately Robert signaled the waiter for their check. Leaving her dinner half eaten, Amber silently got in the car. Somehow the evening had gone flat. Neither of them could find anything to say that would break the uncomfortable silence surrounding them on the way to Amber's home.

Why can't things stay the way they used to be? Amber's heart asked rebelliously. Why do we have to grow up and worry about who to love? Why . . . why . . . why?

Robert's thoughts were churning along the same line. Why did Sam Reynolds have to come here, anyway?

Neither Robert nor Amber had answers to their inner turmoil as they reached the Crossroads Clinic. As she watched the little red taillight disappear in the murky evening, Amber turned sharply into the house, slamming the door behind her. She wanted a good cry, but didn't know what she would be crying for! Totally disgusted with herself she fed Tawny, a constant reminder of Robert's kindness.

If Robert admired Crystal so much, let him have her! Fine thing, it had only been a few weeks since he swore undying love to Amber. Fickle, that's what men were, fickle! She knew she was being unreasonable, but she didn't care. First Sam, now Robert!

Whatever it was that Crystal had, it certainly worked. This thought didn't help much either and it was a thoroughly miserable young nurse who forced herself to stand under a stinging shower, which somehow eased the pain in her heart.

Out on the highway, Robert was equally miserable. What had he done wrong? In his unconceited masculine way, it never once entered his head that his approval of Crystal could upset Amber. If it had, he would have dismissed it immediately. Amber knew he loved her, nothing could change that. He pulled into the driveway and wearily made his way upstairs. It had been a long day. Women, I'll never understand them. With that profound thought he dropped into bed and was asleep, determined to set things right with Amber the next day.

CHAPTER 11

Robert's plan to see Amber the next day was destined to fail. He was called for unexpected surgery that morning and it left him no time to think of personal matters. His patient was a small girl whose appendix was red-hot, on the point of bursting. As he carefully incised the distended abdomen, probed, and gently lifted and tied off, concern filled his face. If peritonitis set in this child was going to be in trouble. He lifted the swollen appendix out and dropped it into a basin. As it slid along the smooth sides, it burst open. They had been just in time!

Perspiration stood out on his forehead as he motioned his assistant to take over. He hadn't realized what tension he had felt until it was all over. Cindylou would be all right. The nicest part of medicine is assuring parents their child will be fine.

"She can go home for Christmas," he

promised. "That's two days away. I'm sure she will be well enough, if you see she takes it easy."

When they had gone he stood in the waiting room. Christmas! What would it mean for him and Amber? Soberly he watched the little family getting into the car. What would it be like to have Amber with him making plans for a family, coming home together after days of satisfying work in the country they loved so well? Suddenly, to the amazement of a passing R.N., the usually dignified Dr. Robert Meacham grabbed her and with a restrained warwhoop waltzed her around the little waiting room, finishing with an elaborate bow.

"Merry Christmas!" he told her, a broad grin covering his whole face. Leaving the nurse staring as if he had taken leave of his senses, the doctor called his office.

"Any pressing appointments?" He waited a moment, then said, "Good! Everyone must be out shopping. I'm going to take some time off this afternoon. I'm going shopping, too." There was nothing in the prosaic words to make his receptionist feel Christmasy, yet for some unexplainable reason she felt the way Christmas bells and holly and manger scenes usually made her feel. Smiling, she turned from the phone, vigorously attacking a mountain of reports. Maybe without Dr. Meacham there she could make inroads on that pile of work. She had Christmas shopping to do, too, and when she finished the doctor had told her she could hang out the closed sign and go.

Robert's heart was pounding as he made his way to the best jewelry store in LaGrande. It took time to work his way through the crowds of laughing holiday shoppers, but at last succeeded in getting the attention of the busy clerk at the ring counter.

It took a long time to make his selection. He didn't want any traditional ring, not for Amber. If he was going to offer himself, it would be with the most beautiful ring he could find. His selection was perfect. A yellow diamond shone pure and clear from its home nest of tiny white diamonds in a gold setting. It was gorgeous. Satisfied, he pocketed it and drove home. It had started to snow. A White Christmas was on its way.

During supper Robert was preoccupied, barely tasting the delicious dinner his housekeeper had prepared. He was happy to see that Charlie Vickers was eating with a healthy appetite. The day after Christmas he would take Charlie out to the Carters. They had been agreeable to his staying with them until a permanent home was found. Ignoring the disappointment in the boy's eyes he told him,

"I have to go out for a while. I won't be gone too long." He knew Charlie would have liked to go with him, but tonight's errand was a one-man job. He had made up his mind. He was going to offer the Christmas ring to Amber tonight. He refused to think what the consequences might be. At least it would show Amber how much he really cared. If she chose elsewhere, he would continue living, but the joy of daily life would be gone. He had his work, yet tonight, even the longed-for accomplishments he had dreamed of as a child didn't seem enough. He wanted Amber. Amber, with her dancing eyes and golden-brown hair! Amber, whose spirit embodied beauty as well as her face! Amber, who could lift him to the seventh heaven if she accepted. His heart beat with anticipation mixed with dread. He carefully felt of the tiny box in his breast pocket, thrilling at the ring's beauty, so suitable for the girl, then frowned as he noticed the clinic ahead was dark and still.

Strange, Amber hadn't had many evening calls lately. It was so dark and the weather so uncertain that she had been trying to avoid them. He waited in front of the little gate until the car was cold and still she didn't come. Where could she be?

When he arrived home, in a somewhat subdued mood, it was after eleven. Well, by now surely she was there. He could at least call. Smothering his disappointment he dialed the Crossroads Clinic, but there was no answer. Fear shot through him. Maybe she was with Sam. His heart sank. Would his rival get ahead of him at this late date, with the ring bought? The lopsided grin facing him in the bathroom mirror restored his sense of humor. As hard as it was snowing now, she couldn't have gone to the Carters, so she wouldn't be with Sam! His spirits lifted. He would call her first thing in the morning and ask her out. It was Christmas Eve the next night, what a perfect time! Charlie was going to spend the night with the Mitchells, and Robert's housekeeper was off for the evening. He was free to be with Amber.

The next morning just before leaving for his office, Robert called the clinic. No answer. He frowned at the instrument, replaced it on the stand, then redialed. Five, ten, twelve times. Amber was not there. Must have had an early call, he reasoned, but just to make sure he called Dr. Mitchell.

"No, I don't know exactly where Amber is," his assistant stated. "But I'm pretty sure she must have stayed over with the Kincaids. Little Amber Lee was croupy and they wanted Amber to come if she could. She went up yesterday morning. I suppose she and Sally May got to visiting and didn't notice the snow starting. You know it's hard to get out of there, even with Amber's snowshoes."

Reassured, Robert hung up and started to his office. Yet somehow he had a presentiment that all was not as it should be. He shrugged it off, but by three o'clock his office had cleared out and it came back to him. Dialing the clinic, he asked for Dr. Mitchell.

"Heard anything of Amber?"

"No, and I'm beginning to worry a little. Tried to call the Kincaids but the line is down. I know they would be plowed out by now — it hasn't snowed much today. She should have come back."

Robert was careful to keep his own concern under control. "Maybe I'll take a run out there. Wait, before I go, check Amber's place and see what all is gone. Did she take extra clothes?"

It seemed only a moment before Dr. Mitchell was back to the phone. "No, just her heavy coat, snowshoes, and medical kit. She wasn't planning on any other calls that I know of."

Promising to call the Mitchells when he found Amber, Robert hurried home, put on the oldest, warmest things he could find and got in his winter-equipped station wagon. While it couldn't equal Amber's jeep for maneuverability, still it could go anywhere a plow had been and a lot of places one hadn't.

He couldn't understand why Amber wasn't home. Stopping by the Crossroads Clinic, he found Dr. Mitchell just closing up. Looking into the older man's eyes he told him, "I'll find her."

Dr. Mitchell shook his head, looking at the sky. "Looks like more snow." He hesitated, then added, "I called the Carters. They haven't seen her. Neither have any of her usual patients in the outlying districts. She must be at the Kincaids'."

The dark-eyed doctor before him seemed to grow older. "She has to be."

"So that's the way it is!" Dr. Mitchell clasped Robert's hand warmly. "Are congratulations in order?"

"I wish they were!" Robert laughed

shortly. "Right now I just want to find her."

The miles to the Kincaids' home seemed longer than ever before. Little did Robert notice the dazzling brilliance of the sun on the snow, except to put on sunglasses against the glare. His energy was directed at checking the tragic scenes conjured up in a too-vivid imagination. When he pulled into the Kincaids' his heart sank. There was no jeep or sign of Amber.

The happy greeting on Sally May's face died at his look of concern.

"Why, what's wrong, Dr. Meacham?"

"Amber," he whispered hoarsely. "Where's Amber?"

Genuine puzzlement filled the woman's face. "Amber? She left here just after lunch yesterday. I begged her to stay, but she was worried about the weather, said it looked like snow, and she didn't want to be snow-bound for Christmas, not even with us! She should be home . . ." Her voice trailed off, horror filling her expression. "You mean she never got there?"

Robert could only shake his head mutely.

"Maybe she stopped by somewhere else," Sally May offered helpfully. "You know her, always helping people. She really is a god-send to the people of this country."

"I know," Robert agreed quietly. "But,

Sally May, we called all her usual patients." Turning to Mark, who had just come up from the barn, he asked, "How long since you plowed out your road?"

Mark's hands clenched and unclenched, betraying his nervousness and worry. "Just a couple hours ago. Noticed the phone line was down, so I went on down the road and reported it. No sign of Amber then. But," he added soberly, "last night's snow would have covered the tracks. Must have gotten over a foot of it."

Again Robert felt that strange presentiment. Something was tugging at his subconscious, struggling to break through, something that could tell him about Amber. He tried to concentrate, to force it to come clear, but it was no use. Whatever it was remained elusive, annoying, undiscovered.

"I'll go back to town and get some of them to help hunt," he said, but Mark shook his head. "No need for that. The Christmas Eve candlelight/carol service is on for tonight. Folks will be coming in for that. We can get all the help we need."

But where can we begin? Robert thought despairingly. The world around them was a world of white, broken here and there by giant trees holding gigantic snowy weights in their branches. The blue sky had become overcast again, predicting more snow. Suppose Amber's jeep had gone off the road? Last night had been bitterly cold. How could she live through that, especially if she had been thrown out? He gritted his teeth. He had thought he knew what it was to love her before, but now, in the face of what could be imminent peril, that love was a mere shadow compared to the raging tide of emotion he felt.

"Oh, Amber," he groaned as he drove back down to the main highway. Then he prayed.

"God, take care of her. This is Christmas Eve, birthday of your Son. Take care of Amber." He didn't realize he had spoken aloud until Mark's voice pierced his misery.

"He will, Robert, He will." There was calm assurance in his voice. "God wouldn't let someone needed as much as Amber die in the storm, not in this country she knows and loves so well. He just wouldn't." Something in the simple trust turned Robert's world back rightside up. Taking one gloved hand from the steering wheel, he gripped Mark Kincaid's outstretched hand with an iron clutch, wordlessly thanking him for his belief.

Shocked faces greeted Mark's announcement to the candlelight/carol worshippers who had gathered so happily. Gone was the laughter. White faces, heads bowed in prayer, tears here and there, held sway for a few minutes. Then every man and boy present was stepping forward, ready to search for Miss Amber, or Dr. Mackenzie's girl, as some of them called her. Up and down the valley they knew and loved her and there wasn't a person there who wouldn't have given all they had for her to be safe.

Sam looked into Crystal's eyes. "I am going with them." She smiled tremulously.

"Of course you are, Sam. And find her! We all love her so much!" Sam saw the deep hurt behind the beautiful eyes and as he plunged out into the growing storm with the others that look sank deep into his heart, glowing there like a precious sapphire. He had no time to analyze his sudden surge of feeling for Crystal, or to compare it with the almost worshipful feelings he held for Amber. He must be with the others to find Amber. And as Sam Reynolds, the cynic, the nonbeliever, stumbled in the darkness now lit by many lanterns, he found himself praying to a previously unknown being.

"Take care of her. If you are there, take care of Amber." The words did not reach his conscious level, yet they were there and became a part of him throughout the long dark night they looked for traces of Amber.

All night long they searched. They combed every known path from the Kincaids' to the main road. There was no sign of Amber. She had vanished as completely as though she had never lived. Christmas Day dawned, but no one heeded it. If Miss Amber was dead, what use to celebrate Christmas? She had been the one who made it a wonderful time for some of those who couldn't have afforded to celebrate otherwise. She had also made it a time of worship. Her influence had helped lessen the commercialism and return some of the old-fashioned holiday spirit. Now she was missing.

Sam and Robert were in the same party. As they walked the long hours together they came to know and appreciate one another. Although each had considered the other a rival, their differences were forgotten in the peril facing them now. Either of the men would have been glad to give up any claim to the other if only she could be found. By the early-morning hours they had found a respect for each other that wouldn't have been possible under any other circumstances. Each of them was facing his own crossroads calling. Each of them was confronted with the value of human life, and that life the life of a beloved girl. Once Robert slipped and would have gone down a steep hillside if Sam had not thrown himself to the very edge and held the young doctor with iron hands as he clambered back up the snowy slope.

Dr. Meacham's face was gray with fatigue as the group of men faced one another in the morning light at their meeting place on the road. It only took one look for them to realize their night's searching had been in vain.

"Better go home for some dry clothes and start again," big Tom Carter ordered. The men were drooping with weariness and cold. It was decided to gather back in an hour.

"Come with me," Dr. Meacham told the Carters and Sam. "It's too far for you to go clear home." Gratefully they climbed in the station wagon, shivering together. Granny, Mrs. Carter, and Crystal's eyes were red with weeping but young Billy had the last word.

"Huh! Miss Amber can take care of herself! We'll find her, all right! No old storm could get her."

Sam leaned his tired head against the side of the station wagon. "Now, if this was one of my stories I'd just write her out of her predicament," he mused aloud. Again that strange prickling under Robert's skin, the sense of being on the verge of something struck him. But again it refused to solidify.

Never had home looked so good to Robert as he led his unexpected Christmas guests into his home. What a difference from the way he had hoped Christmas Day would be spent. He was ashamed of the thought as he looked at the drooping Carter family, gathered in front of the fireplace with its welcoming blaze. He was touched by the readiness with which these people had given up their own Christmas for Amber.

Just as they were getting warmed and thawed out the door burst open. Dr. Mitchell was rudely shoved out of the way by Charlie Vickers, whose eyes mirrored his fright. Running to Robert, he grabbed his arm and shook him.

"He's got her! He's got her!"

Robert stared at him flabbergasted, part of his mind registering the fact that Charlie was using his now-healed arm as easily as the other, even while the words refused to have meaning.

"Who's got her?"

Swallowing what sounded like a quick sob the teenager shook Robert's arm again,

"Vagabond Vic, that's who!" Seeing the doubt in Robert's face he turned to face the others, "Some of you were there, you heard him! He said he'd get even. You've looked everywhere else, haven't you? You know Vagabond Vic's isn't all that far from the Kincaids'. He's got her, I know it!"

Something in the boy's voice and white, shaken face clicked. Now Robert knew what it was his subconscious had been trying to tell him.

He caught Sam's eyes over the boy's head. There was an imperceptible nod, then a gleam in his eye that foretold trouble for Vic. Forgotten were the hot drinks, even the dry clothing. Leaving the rest of the Carters behind, Robert, Sam, and Tom Carter headed for the station wagon.

"You aren't going without me," Charlie Vickers stated, and Billy Carter added stoutly,

"Me, neither!"

For a moment the three men stopped, astonished at the force of the words from the two boys, then grimly Robert told them, "All right. Get in. We've got to find Amber as soon as we can. I don't honestly know if Vagabond Vic would hurt her, but that dog of his . . ." His thought was echoed within each of them, particularly Charlie, who knew only too well what the enraged Satan could do. He gulped back an outcry and stonily stared ahead. Billy Carter saw how he felt and held out a very grimy hand.

"It's okay, I'm here." Another time the older boy might have laughed. Now he was only too glad to hold out his own in friendship. He sensed that beneath Billy's freckles there was a great love for Amber, one that would cause him to do whatever necessary to find her. His own heart was warmed by Billy's gesture toward him. It had been a long time since he had let another boy "get through to him," as he would have put it, but Billy was different. In that moment the two became pals.

Once again Robert turned the big wagon off the highway, but this time he went as far up the lane toward Vagabond Vic's as he could. They had brought snowshovels, and all of them shoveled, Billy and Charlie keeping up their share with the men. But Robert's heart within him was as cold as the beautiful stones in the Christmas ring he had forgotten to take from his shirt pocket before they started the search for Amber. She was in greater danger at Vic's than if she had spent the night fighting the elements of the snowbeaten land. The thought haunted him as he shoveled furiously, and at last they could see a dim light in the distance. Suppressing a shiver, Robert started forward, almost sick at what they might find.

CHAPTER 12

Amber had no way of knowing when she left the Kincaids' farm and drove off into the deepening gray afternoon that she was on the brink of the most unusual and by far the most dangerous escapade she had ever encountered. If she had been, perhaps she would never have stopped at the entrance to Vagabond Vic's country lane. Some irresistible force had slowed the jeep. Was it the threat of a storm, the kind of day she loved? A few flakes, more daring than the deluge to follow, had already drifted down. A small brown rabbit, eyes shining, eyed her for a moment, then scuttled into the underbrush. One lone snowbird sang a few notes, then as if the threatening darkness was too much, slid out of sight into a bush.

Amber smiled at the gloomy world. After a visit at the Kincaids' even the darkest of days could never appear gloomy. Besides, there was something in the air that smelled like Christmas. The dying light only seemed to enhance it.

With another smile at her fancies, Amber started to climb back into the jeep when she heard it. Far in the distance came a dog's bark. There was a note of despair in it. For a moment fear held Amber in her tracks. Dogs only howled like that when there was trouble present. She stared down the empty, overgrown lane to Vagabond Vic's, listening intently, wondering if she had imagined it. No, there it was again. Mournful, forsaken, a howling that sent chills up and down her spine.

Quickly she stepped into the jeep and started on her way, when once more that strange sound cried out, seeming to beckon her to what she knew not, yet calling for help. She drove down the road a little way, then stopped and turned. Odd that her father's teachings should come to her now! For a moment she felt she must go back and see what was wrong. Suppose the animal was caught in a trap? The thought made her shudder. Most of the ranchers used means other than the cruel, steel-jawed traps, but there were a few left.

When she reached the crossroads back to Vagabond Vic's Amber stopped. What could she do if it were Vic's dog Satan caught in the trap? No one could get close enough to help the beast. Yet that same feeling of being at a mental as well as physical crossroads seemed to tell her, Amber, you won't rest if you don't see what can be done. If the dog is in a trap, at least you can go tell Vic. That is, if he will let you near enough the cabin to tell him anything! Doubt assailed her, but not enough to hold her back. Her chin was at a determined tilt, her eyes steady as she plunged into the small road. It had started to snow in earnest now, and it was sticking. No help for that. The howls had grown louder now, and she speeded up as much as she dared. The lane was so rough it would be easy to hit a chuckhole that could nearly swallow her, she thought to herself nervously.

When she reached the small clearing just a little way from Vic's shack, a strange sight met her wondering gaze. Satan, as she had guessed, was firmly caught in a steel trap. She could see the poor, cut paw that was causing the anguished cry for help. But stranger still was the figure crouched in front of him, vainly trying to release the spring and free the dog.

A nondescript coat hung open over red flannel underwear. The coat gave evidence of hard service and of being hastily donned.

An old worn stocking cap covered the man's head, rundown boots protected his feet from the muddy yard. But the oddest thing of all, completely out of place on the wrinkled, battered visage, were the tears falling unashamedly down Vagabond Vic's face.

Robert's words came back to her: Vic loved the dog. It was the only thing he really cared about. Amber's heart warmed at the sight of a spark of goodness in the wicked old man and she was immediately out of the jeep and at his side.

Satan's eyes were glazed with pain — he seemed not to notice the stranger who had knelt beside him.

"Let me help," the girl told the old reprobate. "Get me a stout stick. We can pry the trap open."

There wasn't a sound from the old man as he meekly obeyed. All his former arrogance was gone. Between them they managed to lift the heavy spring and lift the dog free. After carrying him into the dirty shack, Vic laid him on what must be the bed, a pile of boughs underneath a worn spring and dirty mattress, with a faded, ripped quilt for a covering.

Amber looked about, dismayed. Filth was everywhere. She needed something clean, a place to work. Then she remembered there was a pile of newspapers in the jeep. Quickly she ran to the vehicle and returned with her medical case and the papers. She spread them on the floor and put her bag on it. At least it would be clean!

"Is there any hot water?" Her voice was crisp, her nurse's training standing her in good stead. Vic hurriedly poked up the fire in the blackened fireplace and brought her a steaming kettleful. She tempered it, then using antiseptic, bathed the wound.

"It's going to have to be stitched," she told Vic. His face turned white under the coat of dirt, but he only nodded. They wrapped Satan in a blanket, and Vic held him while Amber took the necessary stitches to repair the damaged paw. Surprisingly he gave them little trouble. This in itself worried Amber. With Satan's temperament, it showed how badly hurt he really was.

When she had bandaged the paw, she sank back on the pile of newspapers, completely worn out. They hadn't taught her how to stitch in training, that was the doctor's job! Yet she knew it would have been impossible to get down that rutty road to a vet or even a doctor with the paw in the condition it was. Fortunately she had an excellent antibiotic dressing with her and had applied it liberally.

Amber turned to Vic. Now that it was over, she had better be going. Anxiously she gazed out the dirty window. It was really snowing. She hadn't realized how long she had spent just getting Satan taken care of. It was going to be a struggle even with the jeep to make a few of the turns on the way to the road. She stood, started to speak to Vic, then exclaimed, "Why, you're sick!"

The old man nodded. In the excitement of taking care of Satan, Amber had ignored the hoarse cough and flushed face. Now she saw the old man was really ill. Her heart sank. What could she do?

"We must get you and Satan to the hospital," she told Vic.

He only shook his head. "Won't make it around the big bend."

She knew there was truth in his words. But how could she care for a patient here? For a moment she felt she was going to be sick herself, then a few words from her father's poem came to her. The "right way" was to do all she could for both man and dog. In fact, it was the only way open to her. She opened the front door, noticing how dark and snowy it was, and brought in everything from the jeep she might need. Every time she went out it seemed colder. It would be best to have whatever there was available on hand.

After much persuasion and with almost frazzled nerves, Amber finally succeeded in getting the old man to let her move Satan to one side of the bed while he reluctantly got in the other. That racking cough seemed to have weakened his terrible tongue as well as his physical condition and at last he just gave in. He made her go outside while he put on his other underwear, which she doubted was any cleaner than his present garb, and got in bed.

When Amber checked his temperature she found it even worse than she had expected. It stood over 102 and in the midst of that unbelievably dirty shack Amber didn't even know where to start. She did have some penicillin tablets with her, and at the risk of losing her nursing license if he chose to sue her later for giving medication without a doctor's orders, she gave him what she knew would help, if anything could. She couldn't tell if it was the beginning of pneumonia or just one of the new virus flu strains, but she could at least treat the symptoms. Maybe the next day would bring a relief in the weather.

By now Vic was so ill he didn't care what she did, so valiantly Amber set to work to help her patient. He was no longer just a dirty, objectionable old man to her. He was a suffering human being, a patient who relied on her to help. Without her he could easily die in this shack in the mountains.

There was little enough to work with and Amber found herself going back to basics. Without clean cloths to bathe and cool the fever, Amber made do with the white blouse she had worn under her pullover sweater. There was plenty of water, both hot and cold. She rigged up a makeshift steam tent to relieve some of the congestion by using an old piece of plastic that had been in the jeep, and by midnight she was relieved to find Vic's temperature had gone down a degree.

Unable to sit still, Amber systematically began to clean the cabin. Neither of her patients was awake enough to object, and bit by bit she got through the top layer of dirt, anyway! All the dirty dishes were washed, the floor had been swept and scrubbed, even a hearty broth composed of various vegetables she had discovered in the leanto adjoining the house was simmering on the back of the fireplace over the coals when morning came. Tired to the bone, Amber checked on her patients again, then too weary to care, bundled up in her heavy coat and curled up on a pile of newspapers on the floor. Not once had she remembered it was Christmas Eve!

She was awakened by a faint whine and saw Satan feebly trying to stand on three legs. He had managed to work his way off the bed and was looking at her curiously. Perhaps the memory of her help had softened him, for as she turned he only backed away a little, but didn't snarl.

Quietly she rose from her uncomfortable bed on the floor, ladled off a little of the broth, cooled it, and broke into it some pieces of hard bread she had found in the cupboard. One end had been moldy, but she cut it off and discarded it, frugally deciding to keep the rest. It was hard to tell when they could get out. As far as she knew no one looked after Vic, and no one knew where she was. It would be several days before she could leave them and go out to the main road.

Satan eyed her mistrustfully as she set the bowl of food on the floor within his reach, but his hunger was too much. After a few disdainful sniffs he wolfed it down, then retreated to the far corner and watched her. Amber hoped his paw would be all right. So far at least he hadn't let her get close enough to check it, but the bandage was still in place.

It was a strange day. By now Amber remembered it was Christmas. What a travesty! If it hadn't been so lonely, with only the heavy breathing of the old man and the fixed stare of the dog, Amber would have laughed at the whole situation. They had had such big plans. The Mitchells wanted Robert and her to join them. What would they think? There was no way she could possibly let them know.

In the hours of waiting and watching, hoping and praying for the sick man, Amber learned to know herself better than she ever had before. She thought again of Crystal's assurance that if you loved someone, it was enough just to be with him. She took her feelings out in that lonely, dark cabin and faced them squarely. Attracted to Sam, yes. Willing to turn her back on this country and her work, no. When she had finally decided that, her mind automatically turned to Robert. A strange feeling filled her. He would understand how she felt. He could share her feelings even now if he knew what she was doing. A steady glow began to fill her. She knew now the friendship she had felt for Robert was much more than that. Dreaming, she thought of what life with him would hold. Work, happiness, sometimes hardship. Interrupted outings because of being needed, but joy of service.

A low moan recalled her to the present. Checking Vic's temperature again, Amber's heart sank. After all her work, it had started to rise again. Patiently she bathed him in as cool a water as she dared. It wouldn't do to expose him too much. The hours passed and she was again rewarded by a drop in temperature. About noon he opened his eyes and looked at her strangely. He started to speak, but she cut him off with a motion.

"Don't talk." Seeing his wild gaze around the cabin, she pointed to Satan, asleep in front of the bed. "He's all right."

A faint trace of what would have been a smile in anyone but Vic crossed the pallid features. Quietly she brought a bowl and fed him as much soup as he would take.

"Christmas dinner." He looked at her quickly, a spark of interest in his sunken eyes, then turned over and slept again. Somehow the flicker of light determined Amber more than ever. She would see he got well! Grimly she attacked the cabin again. This time she got below the second level of grime, and when she was finished, the place looked almost livable. She even washed the window. As she was putting the faded, dirty curtain back up she saw movement outside in the snow. Holding her breath, she peered harder, but couldn't make out what it was. A human? Then why was he skulking across the yard toward the cabin? Why didn't he come to the porch? Now the figure was by the jeep, muffled against the cold, examining the vehicle.

Satan's growl filled the cabin, and he took a menacing step toward the door. Amber's fear was eclipsed by what could happen. Casting a worried glance at her patient, who had roused and was attempting to sit up in bed, she made up her mind. If someone took the jeep, they were stranded. She felt in the pocket for the keys, blood draining from her face. How could she have left them in the ignition? Clearly she remembered how when she had arrived worry over the dog had shoved any other thoughts aside. The keys were in the jeep.

With a jerk she pulled open the warped door and stepped outside.

"What are you doing there?" she demanded, her voice shaking in spite of herself.

Before the figure could straighten and reply, something shot past Amber. It was amazing how fast Satan could run on three legs, but run he did, straight for the man who had wheeled to Amber when she spoke.

As the two went down in a heap, Amber saw to her horror the man was Robert!

CHAPTER 13

For a moment Amber was too frozen to move, then her voice rose in a piercing cry.

"Satan!" Afterward she would never know whether the dumb beast recognized her voice or if it had been the sheer desperation in her call that caused him to pause an instant, just long enough for Sam Reynolds to envelop him in the heavy coat he had jerked off when Satan attacked.

Like a homing pigeon Amber flew to Robert's side. "Are you all right?" she demanded, shaking him furiously, tears streaming down her white face.

Something in the man's eyes kindled. The dawn of hope from Amber's tone caused him to catch his breath before answering quietly, "I'm fine. What about you? What are you doing here?"

His tone brought Amber back to reality. Her story tumbled out as she led Robert into the transformed shack.

"I had to come," she finished simply. The doctor didn't reply but the look he gave her showed he understood perfectly. She had come to a crossroads and chosen the right path, even as her father would have done.

There was grave concern in Robert's face as he looked down at Vic. Despite all Amber's efforts, he was still a very sick man, who needed hospitalization as soon as possible. Striding to the door, Dr. Meacham called out, "Sam, Tom! Can we get the jeep out? We've got a mighty sick patient in here."

Sam looked up from the struggling Satan, who he had managed to tie to a porch post.

"We'll get him out." There was determination in his level gaze. The same feeling was echoed in Tom Carter's rugged countenance and reflected even in Billy's and Charlie's faces.

Without further conversation the men began shoveling with all their might while Amber did what she could to prepare the old man for an extended hospital stay. Finally she gave up — it was hopeless. She knew someone would find something clean and decent for Vic when the time came for him to come home. Dr. Mitchell kept a ready supply of worn but clean clothing for such occasions. She would borrow from him.

"What about the dog?" Billy's anxious question interrupted the steady pace they had set. The little band of workers had nearly reached Robert's station wagon when he spoke. It had been a hard afternoon's work, but Vic held his own. It would only be a short while before they could get him to where he would be properly cared for.

There was a blank look on the men's faces as they headed back to the cabin. What could they do with Satan? The dog, although weakened, had certainly proved he could not be approached.

"Let me try," Billy begged. Something about the big ugly dog fascinated him. At first they wouldn't hear of it, yet they were nearly ready to go.

Taking a piece of bread and soaking it in the leftover broth, Billy threw small pieces to where Satan was tied, talking to him in a boyish treble all the while.

"It's okay, fella, I won't hurt you. All you have to be is a little friendly. Can't go through life being mean. Come on, fella, it's okay." Little by little the boy stepped closer.

"Careful!" Amber's whisper stopped Billy in his tracks, but after a moment's hesitation he resumed his slow walk. Finally he was within reach of the dog. Satan looked him over carefully, then to the utter amazement of all, wagged his tail. Billy reached out his mittened hand and very slowly patted the dog's head. After a short bark, the dog's mouth opened and he licked Billy's hand!

Amber gasped. She wouldn't have believed it could happen if she hadn't seen it with her own eyes. Billy's eyes glowed. Somehow he had felt he could win Satan over if he only tried.

When they took Vic out to the jeep, carefully holding him as best they could and wrapping him up against the cold, he opened his eyes. There was a bewildered look in them mingled with pain.

"Satan?" he croaked, looking wildly around. When he saw Billy with the dog that almost-smile touched his features and he closed his eyes again.

It was decided that Robert, Amber, and Vic would go in the jeep. It should finish breaking the trail enough for the others to get the station wagon in and pick up Billy and Satan. They would take Satan to an animal hospital while his master was being cared for in LaGrande. But first of all, when Robert and Amber got to the hospital, they would call off the search! In the concern over the two patients, the reason for their all being there had been eclipsed. Christmas

Day was nearly over, and what a day it had been!

Robert's mind was torn between concern for his patient, the look he had seen on Amber's face when Satan attacked, and the ring still securely held above his heart. Amber was tired, but intensely happy. How could she have escaped knowing what her real feelings were? If Robert had been badly hurt by Satan, life wouldn't have been worth living.

Sam, busily engaged in directing Tom Carter as he drove the wagon along the still tricky lane, was reflecting on Amber's face. He knew now this was where she belonged. Strangely, it didn't hurt so much as he had thought it would. Could it be that pair of green eyes and genuine concern of Crystal's had cushioned what would have been bitter disappointment a few days ago? He must think about it. He considered the strange events of the previous evening and day. He could hardly wait to write the chief, or to put down notes for his own story! He could weave it into the thread of his book. Suddenly he was aware that they had reached the cabin.

Now the problem was to load Satan. It was simpler than they thought. Charlie piled in the front seat between Sam and Tom Carter, then Billy, talking softly again, led Satan to the rear opening, and enticed him in with more food. The sick dog laid down almost gratefully and put his head on Billy's foot. He had done his duty protecting the homestead, now he could rest, was his attitude.

The two boys looked at each other with respect. Charlie knew he could never have handled Satan like Billy had done. For one thing, he had hated the dog too long. Even dogs could feel your friendship, Billy had said. Satan had no reason to love Charlie. With Billy it was different. He had seen something in the dog no one else had, and had reached him because of that insight.

Although Christmas came late, it was a joyful one. Up and down the valley, to the lake, to the smallest towns the news traveled. Miss Amber was a heroine. Gossip was rampant. It ranged from the tale she had fought off singlehanded both the dog and Vagabond Vic, to the story she was now in the hospital with a broken leg, suffering from exposure! A few well-placed telephone calls dispelled the fears, and the different families settled down to a well-earned Christmas rest. That is, all except Robert and Amber. They were fighting the Grim Reaper. Even though they had done everything very carefully, old Vic's life hung in

185

the balance. The hours passed, Christmas Day had come and gone, yet still they fought. What had been the flu had turned to pneumonia, as Amber had feared.

"It's only because of your care he hasn't died already," Robert told Amber when they were taking a short break. Neither had slept the night before, and the strain had taken its toll. Yet they wouldn't dream of someone else caring for Vic. They felt he had grown to be part of them, someone to do all they could for as long as it was necessary.

Amber slipped into a chair in the corner of the room about two o'clock. The night shadows were too much, she couldn't keep awake. Robert gently spread a quilt over her, but as the morning light just began to creep over the snow-covered world he roused her.

"Amber." He couldn't go on, he didn't need to. She knew.

"He's gone?"

"Yes. I wanted to come for you, but it happened too rapidly. Evidently the strain was too much for his heart. Just before he died he opened his eyes and smiled.

" 'I'm sorry. Tell her . . . I'm sorry.' "

Amber couldn't speak. She had come to feel so personally toward him, this down-and-out relic of humanity. What had brought him to such a hatred of the world and its people she didn't know. But in the last day and a half she had learned to care about him. Now he was gone. It was too much. Despite all her careful training not to get emotionally involved with her patients, she dropped her head in her arms and sobbed. In it was all the heartbreak of a wasted life, a little feeling of shame that she had come close to not helping, and the sadness of those who work to preserve life, only to see it slip away as they stand helplessly by.

Robert looked at her in silence. Her grief was too deep even for him to intrude. He thought again of what he had planned for the day just past. That would wait. It was good for her to cry. For only a second his hand lay on the shining hair, tenderness in his eyes, then he stepped into the hall, telling the morning-duty nurse to leave the room alone for a time.

Amber didn't know how long she cried, but at last she roused. In spite of everything she felt better, and a longing to see Vagabond Vic once more seized her. Stepping to the bed and drawing the sheet aside, she looked into the still features. A great gladness filled her. There was peace and dignity in death that Vic's life had lacked. She was happy she had looked. That would be the way to remember Vic. True, he had been a wicked, vicious old man. Yet he was a part of creation. She could respect him as part of that creation, and remember the good she knew of him. Her father had once told her, "Any man who a dog loves can't be all bad." The thought came back to her now, and she stooped and kissed the wrinkled cheek, perhaps the first kiss he had been given since babyhood.

Quietly she drew the sheet up again.

Robert was waiting for her at the nurse's station.

"You need rest," he told her firmly, holding her arm as they went down the icy steps to the jeep. "I'm taking you home."

Never had home looked so good to Amber as then! Tawny, who had been fed but unloved for the past two days greeted her with a warm rattle of purring, and Robert had a fire going almost before she knew it. Too tired to eat, she went straight to bed, leaving him to lock up and get to his own home. Now that it was all over there was the inevitable letdown. He needed rest as much as Amber.

The Carters had stayed over at Robert's home, made welcome by Charlie in the doctor's absence. They had had a grand time foraging in the refrigerator and making inroads on several pies in the freezer. When Robert arrived home, Crystal and Mrs. Carter had breakfast ready and it was a welcome sight. He realized he hadn't eaten for over twenty-four hours, but made up for it! Waffle after waffle disappeared until at last even Billy and Charlie could eat no more.

Billy's eyes got big when Robert told them Vic was gone.

"What about Satan?" was his first question. Robert had anticipated it.

"He will be okay with the vet for a few days, then . . ." He looked inquiringly at Tom.

Billy's eyes glistened. "Can I, Dad? Can I have him?"

Tom didn't know what to say. In spite of the fact Satan had accepted Billy, he was still a dangerous beast. How could he consent? Yet he could see his son had his heart set on it.

"Why don't we wait and see how Satan acts at the animal hospital?" Sam suggested. He was rewarded by a brilliant smile from Billy and a look of relief from Tom. If the vet said it was safe, then they would take Satan home the next week when they came in.

Charlie was excitedly getting his things together. Since the Carters were there now, it had been decided he would go home with them. That way he could be enrolled in school right after the holidays. Something in him had responded to "Mom" Carter, as she had asked him to call her, and Crystal was the prettiest thing he had ever laid eyes on! Well, he amended mentally, almost the prettiest. No one could beat Miss Amber for looks! As for Billy, Tom, and Sam, Charlie had learned to respect them fully.

Now that Vic was dead Charlie determined to forget the hatred he had felt for the old man. He knew it was wrong to harbor bad feelings, he had learned that from Robert's example. Robert, who had been in such danger, yet who would stay up all night to care for a worthless old man! His heart beat with joy. He hoped the foster-placement board never found him anywhere to stay — then he could be with the Carters!

All in all it was a happy but tired crew that piled into the Carter car for the trip home to Lostine. Probably they would have more shoveling to do in the entrance to their own road. But what did it matter? Word had been given out that a special New Year's watch night would be held, in thankfulness for Amber's safe return, and folks were looking forward to it immensely.

At the Crossroads Clinic Amber and her little cat slept the clock around. The clinic was closed until after New Year's, except for emergencies. Amber was taking the time to help the Mitchells give the rooms a fresh paint coat. This is where Sam found her when he came down the next evening, determined to have a long talk with her. He had experienced feelings never before known since coming to her land. Now it was time to open his heart, as she had opened hers about her father, and tell Amber exactly where he stood — and how much he had changed since his fall arrival. He knew it would be a difficult interview, but it had to be done, and now while they were still caught up in the recent happenings was the time to speak.

CHAPTER 14

Amber climbed down off the ladder after she had applied the last brushful of paint and proudly surveyed her work. The soft yellow certainly did wonders for the waiting room! She was startled by a knock at the door. She grimaced at her mirrored reflection and answered the door.

"Sam! I certainly didn't expect you tonight!"

His grin was amused at her obvious discomfort. "I can see that." Sobering, he said, "I realize I should have called but, Amber, I had to see you." Amber's heart sank at the seriousness of his voice. She led him into the living room and left him to play with Tawny while she quickly cleaned up a bit.

Amber dreaded the coming interview. Her face was flushed as she came back to the fireplace and threw on another chunk.

"It's the heart of your home, isn't it?" Sam asked, with a deep look into the mysteries of the smoke curling upward into the black recesses of the chimney.

"Now that Dad's gone, it is," she responded. It gave him the opening he needed and he turned to face her, the firelight shining on his earnest face, deepening the intensity of his fine eyes.

"Amber, I hardly know how to begin." He was silent for a long time. At last he began to speak, and it was like a dam had burst inside him. He told her of the childhood he had spent, miserably clawing his way up to be someone. He told of the do-gooders and the hypocrites, the well-meaning friends with their advice of a vague religious something, somewhere, mystical, unreal to his searching mind.

"At last I made up my mind there was nothing except what I made life. For several years I felt that way. Then" — he looked into the fire again, as if conjuring up memories — "my chief called me in and handed me an obituary." Amber sat as if turned to stone as he went on. It all came out. His dislike for the assignment. His first feelings as he stood by her father's grave and read the carved inscription on the simple stone.

He went on to tell her of his mixed feelings that first night in the Nez Perce Motel, that it would hurt not only his editor but himself if he found in any way that David Mackenzie was less than the man he seemed to be. His voice became hoarse as he told her how the simple people of the country she loved had begun to show him a way of life he hadn't dreamed existed, where people loved and cared and helped one another. Where people took him in and made him welcome. Where the influence of a man now gone lived on in the lives of his patients.

Amber felt she was being permitted to look into the very depths of Sam Reynolds's soul. Her hands were clasped tightly, her mind intent on every word. Even Tawny's transfer from Sam's lap to her own didn't register. She automatically stroked the soft fur and continued to listen, totally absorbed in the story.

The sharp ring of the phone interrupted the narrative.

"Hello . . . oh, Robert! Fine, thanks. No . . . not tonight, Sam's here . . . I see. All right, tomorrow. Good night."

Sam guessed by the quick color in her face that Robert had misunderstood his presence. He spoke quietly, "I understand, Amber."

She looked at him, amazed. How could he have suspected what she had only recently come to learn herself? Sam smiled gently.

"I think I have always known. And then when Satan jumped Robert, I saw your face."

Amber met his gaze steadily, a joyous light coming to the beautiful eyes when she saw his gaze was clear, untroubled by pain.

"Oh, Sam," she exclaimed, holding out both hands. For a moment he gripped them, then leaned back and took up his story.

"I hadn't realized how much I needed to change perspective until I met you, Amber. My life had been all work, very little play. Then suddenly there you were. I can never deny I learned to love you a great deal." Again he stopped, cleared his throat, then went on.

"Yet as I said, I think I always knew Robert was the one for you. He is born and bred of this country, as you are. I am not." For a long time he was silent.

"I tried to convince myself I could stay here and write and be completely happy. But, Amber, throughout the search for you I realized if I did that it would be only because of my respect for your feelings, not because I believed in it. Then, too, there has been my growing admiration for Crystal." He looked at her humbly.

"I wonder if you can understand how a

person could be so attracted to two people at once?" She only smiled, thinking to herself, How well I know, how very well I know!

"Finally I seem to have it all sorted out. Amber, no matter how far I go, or where, there will be no one who will take your place. Yet that place is not of wife and mother in my house. You have been an inspiration, almost an idol. But most important, you have helped me come to see things as they really are. I fought it. All these weeks I have fought the idea that anyone could live as you and your father did, trusting an Almighty power for daily needs as well as Sunday meetings! When I told Crystal about your father's poem she said something that has haunted me:

" 'David Mackenzie didn't just believe God was real, Sam. He knew it, and lived it, and showed it without ever preaching one word.'

"She was right. I thought of her statement and at last I knew she had to be right. She believed that way too, after the glamour wore off and I saw the real Crystal. Granny and the other Carters believe it, and Robert, and others. But it wasn't until your life was in danger that I could accept it for myself." His voice grew very low.

"All night long while we searched I kept the thought in my mind, 'take care of her, if you are there, take care of her.' It wasn't a prayer, it was just something that kept me going, and I knew the others were feeling the same way. Then when we found you, unharmed, in that awful cabin with that hideous old man, taking care of him and his vicious dog, it all fell into place. You had followed the crossroads calling, too."

Amber was speechless. To think that Sam would feel so was more than she could believe. The cynical reporter who had come to this country was gone. In his place stood a man who had suffered, but who had conquered.

When she recovered enough to speak she asked, "What are your plans?"

Again he met her direct gaze steadily. "My crossroads will take me in another direction. For you and Robert your 'right' direction is here. But for me, I don't really know. I strongly suspect that when spring comes, and my book is written, I too will be faced with 'Two Ways for the Traveler.' Then I will need the strength to choose the right way . . ." He left the sentence unfinished, but Amber supplied the remainder:

". . . to happiness, and to God."

"Perhaps." He smiled slightly. "But if so,

it will be to the kind of God I've found here, unshackled by narrow ideas of 'Sunday Christianity.' "

The fire had died to a few coals before they finished talking, but when Sam rose to leave he couldn't resist boyishly asking, "You don't mind, do you? About Crystal, and about you? I love you both, but in such different ways! Do you think I have a chance with her?"

Amber's unruly tongue longed to reassure him but wisely she held the words in check. "I wouldn't be a bit surprised," she drawled, laughter setting little golden flecks dancing in her eyes. Cocking her head, she glanced at him slantwise. "And no, I don't mind. You see, I just happen to be in the same situation!" Sam's eyes widened. He hadn't thought of it that way.

"I hope my being here doesn't make trouble with Robert," he told her anxiously.

"Of course not," she scoffed, but when he had gone she looked in the mirror for a long time. Would it make a difference? Robert had sounded a little strange on the phone.

Amber saw little of Robert the following week, so there was no chance for explanations. Even if there had been, the times Amber did see him, he was all "Dr. Meacham," not the approachable friend she knew and had come to love deeply. After a few days she began to wonder if he was deliberately avoiding her. Sure, there was a lot of sickness right now, but he had always found time to be with her before. One day she saw him driving by when she was in LaGrande. She started to raise her hand in greeting, but it died on her lips. Her face turned ashen. Perched close beside him on the front seat of the station wagon was Crystal Carter, beautifully bundled up in a bright green coat and stocking-cap outfit. She was laughing up at the doctor, who smiled down at her with real affection in his eyes. Amber had no way of knowing Sam had brought Crystal into town to do some shopping and the doctor had picked them up for a snack. Sam had seen an item in a window and dashed from the car into the store.

All Amber saw was the smile, and the beauty. Somehow the day had lost its luster for her. Dejectedly she climbed into the jeep. She had been so sure that once she discovered how much Robert meant to her her troubles were over! Now she was plunged into the depths of despair again. Had she waited too long? Was this Robert's reaction to finding Sam there when he had called a few nights before?

Poor Sam! Amber's heart went out to him. He had learned to care for Crystal and evidently her change of heart had been only temporary. It appeared she was every bit the flirt she had always been! Yet she had seemed so sincere!

It was all too much for Amber. Determinedly she drove her jeep back to the clinic and spent the rest of the day adding finishing touches to the freshly painted clinic.

Meanwhile Sam had come back to the station wagon and the three had gone for their snack. In his own way Robert was as puzzled as Amber had been. What was going on, anyway? One night he called Amber and Sam was with her, yet now here the man was with Crystal, hanging on her every word! What was wrong with the man? How could he treat Crystal as a rare painting when he was in love with Amber? Or was he? Disgustedly he finished his lunch and abruptly excused himself. There was work to do. He had no time to sit around and watch Sam Reynolds moon. Robert had almost convinced himself that the look Amber had given him at Vic's was born of the moment, worry combined with sisterly affection. His clinic was crowded when he got there, and finally he lost himself in work, but every so often Amber's face would pop into mind. Finally the last patient left. Robert decided that tonight he would offer Amber the ring. He took the small white box from the safe and looked at it tenderly. Even if she only accepted him rebound, he had decided to marry Amber. He would make her happy, and time might heal her feelings for Sam.

If Amber had only known! It would have saved her some very unhappy hours. When Robert called and asked to take her to the New Year's service, his voice was strained, unnatural.

"I have something very important to tell you," he said, and Amber's heart sank. She could almost hear the dull thud as it hit rock bottom.

"I'm sure it will be interesting," she said flatly, biting her lips furiously to keep back the tears crowding up, threatening to choke her.

"I'll pick you up at eight-thirty," he said. That would give him time to offer her the ring, and himself. The service didn't start until nine-thirty and it was only a short drive.

Amber usually took pride in dressing but tonight it was different.

"Why should I care?" she stormily asked her twin in the dresser mirror. "What does it matter? He will come out here, tell me that he and Crystal have discovered they have loved each other 'after all these years,' and he will expect me to tell him how wonderful it is! Well, I can't do it! I just can't do it!" She flung herself, sobbing, on the bed. A tiny voice whispered, Serves you right. You didn't want him all this time, now he's found someone else. Catching sight of a snapshot of her father tucked into the edge of the mirror she brokenly demanded, "What now, Dad? I'm at a crossroads. But I have no choice. What can I do?" The smiling picture seemed to reassure her like nothing else could have done. For a moment she could almost have sworn her father's right eye winked! Was he trying to tell her something? What could it be? She was lost in reverie until the sound of the clock striking eight times reminded her Robert would be there soon.

Lifting the Mackenzie chin, she reached into the closet and pulled out a new yellow skirt and sweater outfit. If she had to face Robert's defection to Crystal she had made up her mind to face it squarely. She brushed the golden-brown hair until it shone, and added an extra touch to the perfume and lipstick. Cold water erased the traces of tears, and she was ready with only five minutes to spare.

Robert caught his breath as she stepped to the door and welcomed him. Again she was a golden girl, the spirit of sunlight. How could he have thought he had a chance? Still he was determined. Seating himself across from her he brought out the little box and said, "Would you like to see the present I bought for someone very special?"

Amber forced herself to take the tiny box and press the spring. Her fingers trembled, and then it opened. The firelight gleamed in the heart of the yellow diamond and the white ones surrounding it shone with starlike brilliance. So this is what he had been doing with Crystal downtown! Why hadn't he given it to her then?

Forcing a disinterested tone she said, "It's very beautiful," and handed it back to him.

Robert looked at her almost diffidently.

"Do you think that certain someone would wear it . . . would promise to be my wife?"

The pain in Amber's heart was almost more than she could bear but she kept her voice light. Yet try as she must, it was impossible to hold back some of her bitterness. To cover up her real feelings she laughed airily.

"Well, you never can tell! Some girls like to flit from flower to flower, but then it is a gorgeous ring," she added condescendingly. The moment the words were out she regretted them. What a terrible thing to do! What if Crystal was fickle? She had had no right to throw it into Robert's face that way.

"I see." There was a white line of pain around Robert's mouth and his eyes were bleak as he pocketed the ring. "Are you ready?" His voice was dull and lifeless. Amber felt like a murderess. Never in all their years of growing up had she seen Robert without the faintest flicker of hope in his eyes.

"I'm sorry . . ." she faltered, but he only said,

"It's all right, Amber. I should have known better than to hope for such a thing." It cut her to the quick. Her blood boiled, first with anger at Crystal, then with shame for her own actions.

The evening wasn't very successful. For totally different reasons neither Robert nor Amber could keep their eyes off Sam Reynolds and Crystal Carter. As the service progressed and it was time to light candles and ring the bell for the new year, Amber stood up.

"Don't let's stay," she whispered. The pain in her heart was too much to bear. She had lost the dearest things on earth to her the past year, first her father, now Robert. It was more than she could do to sit there and then joyfully sing hymns when the new year came. Seeing her glance at Crystal and Sam and interpreting it exactly opposite from what it was, Robert was glad to agree. Silently they drove home through the night. For once even Amber little heeded the full moon and brilliant stars shining down from a cloudless sky overhead. In the distance rose snowcapped mountain peaks, serenely etched against the sky, but in the station wagon there was only the misery of complete misunderstanding between the two who loved each other so much.

CHAPTER 15

When Amber looked back on January and February, they always loomed in her mind as months of misery. Never had she known such pain as assailed her. It didn't help to see Robert growing thinner and whiter each time she saw him. At last she could stand it no longer.

"I'm going away for a while," she told him the first week in March.

"I've been expecting you to go," was his reply. Amber looked at him curiously but didn't respond. There was nothing to say.

Sam was to make a quick trip to Portland. Don Baker wanted to see how things were going. He had asked Amber, Crystal, and Robert if they would be his guests. He had some friends with a lovely inn near the city and would be happy to put them up for the week he needed to be in town. The four of them would have a wonderful time.

Robert declined curtly. The "wonderful

time" sounded like a nightmare to him. He could use the excuse of too much to do easily. He could barely hide his unhappiness as the three drove off. Neither could he understand Amber. If she loved Sam, and by now he knew she must, why would she want Crystal with them every minute? Oh, well, maybe she felt it would be better than if she had gone alone with Sam. It would be quite a time. Don Baker was to have them all up to his mansion one night, they would see some good shows, try new restaurants. If things had been different he would have enjoyed it immensely. It was a long time since he had a vacation. From season to season he had put it off, hoping against hope it could become a honeymoon when Amber was ready. Now that dream was shattered. Maybe he would go on a trip, too. Dr. Mitchell would help out, and he needed the rest.

Sighing, he called in his next patient, irritably wishing mothers would keep their children out of mudpuddles in this treacherous in between winter and spring season.

While Robert was working himself ragged, trying to erase visions of Amber being admired in Portland, Amber herself was caught in a trap of her own making. She had hoped to have time for a little chat with

Crystal, but there was never time. It seemed Sam wanted Crystal with him every minute, and Amber was pretty much left to her own devices. One day she impulsively went down to the *Star* and asked to see the chief. They weren't to dine with him until later that week, but she wanted to see him when others weren't present.

Don Baker's greeting warmed her through and through. Thrusting aside his pile of work, he took her home with him to spend the day. For hours they talked of David Mackenzie, from boyhood escapades to his death and when the day was over, Amber knew she had found a friend who would stand by her always. She had not told him of her own unhappiness, but somehow she felt he knew.

Just before time for her to leave he took her hand.

"Amber, I have come to my crossroads — and I have decided which way is right for me. I am going to offer the editorship to Sam if he will take it, and I think he will. Then I'm going to sell this old ark of a place" — he smiled at her stifled gasp — "and I'm coming to your country. There is an opportunity for a newspaperman there, and I think I can find happiness, perhaps what your father had. I've even chosen the

208

name of my paper — the *Crossroads Courier.* I want to run it for the benefit of people. I already have enough money to outlast me; it doesn't matter if I make a profit."

Wordlessly Amber clutched his hand. She was so glad!

The editor laughed at her confusion. "Guess what?" He sounded like a young boy. "Granny Carter has decided after this winter that she's a lot more comfortable with her family than alone. Says she misses the noise. I am going to buy her cabin and make my home there." His eyes took on a faraway look.

"I remember when David and I were both young, our ambition was to break free, to cut loose from the crowd and find a place where we could 'holler as loud as we wanted' and not bother a soul! That dream came true for him, now it will come true for me."

Amber left wondering. One could never tell what was going on inside another human being. She had glimpsed her father's boyhood friend and his dreams. It brought her own dear father even closer.

While she was in Portland, Amber made it a point to stop by Memorial Hospital. After all those years she didn't know if anyone would remember her father but in this she was mistaken. The Head Nurse, Chief Dietitian, countless others. They knew and remembered David Mackenzie. After a particularly warm interview with the Head Nurse, she put her arm about Amber.

"If you ever want a job, there will be one here for you," she promised. Amber's eyes filled with tears and she started to shake her head but caught herself. If things didn't get better back home she might be glad of the offer. She wouldn't completely close the door.

"I'll remember," she promised, and with another smile the nurse went back to her duties, smiling at the thought of how proud David Mackenzie would be of his lovely daughter. There was the same spirited lift of head, the same contouring of chin. Yes, he would be proud.

Amber returned from Portland even quieter than before. During the days there she had seen that Sam and Crystal were very much in love. Then where did that leave Robert, except out in the cold?

He loved me once, I'll make him love me again, she thought, then a wave of shame swept over her. No, I can't do that. I'm not the type to throw myself at a man, no matter how much life hurts without him. I can only hope and pray that in time he will get over Crystal. There were times when she felt an unutterable longing to go straight to Robert and at least make their friendship right. Yet something held her back. She didn't know how to approach him. If he had seemed angry she would have apologized, but instead he met her every advance of friendship with the same courtesy he bestowed impartially on his many patients.

March gave way to April, then Easter. At least the land looks alive again, Amber thought. Something of the season seemed to cheer her. The long winter was gone. All the bulbs that had lain dormant since fall were sending forth shoots and flowers. Tulips were raising yellow, red, purple, white cups to the sky, eager to catch and store every passing raindrop, each ray of sun. On Easter Sunday Amber visited her father's grave with a huge bouquet of flowers. Tears sprang to her eyes when she noticed the arrangement already there. Nowhere in the valley did such blossoms grow. Well, she knew who had brought them. Robert's tiny flower garden must have been stripped.

She leaned her head against the simple stone and closed her eyes for a moment when she knelt to place her own flowers. It was so peaceful, so untroubled here in the warm sun. She had forgotten how nice it could be just to be silent in the sunlight. Strengthened, she rose and made her way home, to be greeted by Tawny's plaintive meow. No longer any sign of kittenish ways about him. If he got any bigger he would look like a tiger in front of the fireplace!

April days were busy. Amber again resumed her many calls into the outlying areas. The busier her days, the easier the long nights, she discovered. The announcement of Sam and Crystal's engagement didn't help. She had hoped that somehow once it was a fact she and Robert would be on better footing, but it didn't change things. They had asked Amber and Robert to stand up with them, but even that didn't mend the breach.

One day Dr. Mitchell called Amber in when the last patient had gone.

"I'm worried about Robert," he told her, his keen eyes boring into her. Amber gave a start. She had been thinking exactly the same thing. Her face colored but she turned away. What could she say? The droop of her shoulders told Dr. Mitchell more than she realized.

So! he thought to himself. That's it! Then why . . . ? Suddenly he blurted out in his blundering way, well meaning but outspoken, "Aren't you two in love?"

The small voice shook as his nurse replied, "Robert is."

"You mean you don't care?"

"Me!" she said. "It's Crystal he cares for."

"Huh, something wrong with that picture." Dr. Mitchell scratched his head. For a moment a leap of hope filled Amber but it died quickly.

"It's true." She hesitated on the doorstep. "I'm going out to see if I can help the Carters. Granny isn't any too well and all the wedding excitement isn't good for her. She insists on being in everything." For a moment her old eagerness filled her.

"The good thing about the Carters is the way Charlie has fit in. They decided they couldn't give him up and are planning to legally adopt him." She laughed.

"The other thing is Satan, only now he is Bruno instead of Satan. He's become a loving pet to the whole family, believe it or not! As a watchdog he's a total loss — he will eat out of the hand of anyone who brings him anything!"

"Just goes to show what can be done with love," Dr. Mitchell commented. Amber looked at him sharply but there was only innocence on his smooth face.

The Carters were in an uproar. The next night was the rehearsal and Crystal's silver

213

slippers hadn't arrived. Granny couldn't hem her dress until she had them so the length would be right. Crystal had pleased her grandmother very much by insisting she wanted to wear the heirloom dress that had been packed away for years and years.

"Nothing new for me," she giggled to Amber. "I've had so many clothes that I won't need anything for years! It's a good thing. Until we get a little house paid for I don't intend to spend money on myself." It was all settled they would be going back to Portland. Both Sam and Crystal felt this was their "right" path. They would always treasure and come back to the valley, yet there was work to be done elsewhere. Running a paper was a big job and it took big people to do it right. They planned to print as much "good news" as they could, in addition to the daily happenings.

The chief was in his seventh heaven. He would be staying on from the wedding. His assistant would be on duty while Crystal and Sam honeymooned at the Coast for a couple weeks, but Don was free to leave. He had taken a fancy to Billy Carter and Charlie Vickers and they followed him everywhere, promising to take him fishing when summer came and school was out. He was enjoying himself thoroughly.

Without quite knowing how, Amber found Crystal had maneuvered her into Crystal's bedroom. Closing the door and leaning against it, Crystal asked quietly, "Amber, what's wrong between us? That day so long ago when you were here . . . I thought we would be real friends. But something's different." There was a tremor in the blonde girl's voice. "Is it because of Sam? It needn't be. I know he will never have the same feeling for me he does you. I wouldn't want him to. Is that what it is?"

Amber gazed at her, astonished, then her eyes filled with tears.

"It isn't Sam, it's Robert."

Genuine puzzlement was in Crystal's eyes. "Robert? You mean Dr. Meacham?"

"Yes!" Suddenly the whole story burst out of Amber. How she had seen them in LaGrande. How she and Robert had been sitting so close, laughing. How Robert had come later and shown her the wonderful yellow diamond he had selected. How Amber couldn't understand why Crystal would lead Robert on when she loved Sam.

Crystal's expression was horrified. "Amber, you have done Robert a terrible injustice. That ring wasn't for me, it was for you. He bought it the day of Christmas Eve."

Amber stared at her unbelieving. Crystal

215

went on. "The day you saw us we had just dropped Sam off at a store and were driving around the block to come back and pick him up. There weren't any parking spots." She looked at Amber, dead serious.

"Dr. Meacham showed me the ring. The amber ring for an Amber girl. How could you misunderstand?"

Amber couldn't reply. What had she done? When she told Robert his special someone would like to flit from flower to flower. He had thought she referred to herself!

"Oh, Crystal, he'll never forgive me!" she wailed, tears starting. The tiny girl was the stronger of the two at that moment.

"Yes, he will! Get those tears out of your eyes and tell him tonight on the way home from rehearsal! I know he's taking you, he mentioned you were having jeep trouble."

Again Amber stood at a crossroads, but this time there was a neon sign in her heart pointing the way. She flushed with shame — she didn't deserve another chance. What if Crystal was wrong? What if she had hurt Robert irrevocably? It was a chance she would have to take.

Robert was very quiet throughout the rehearsal. When the lovely words of the familiar service brought tears to Amber's eyes he grimly clenched his teeth, but on the way home he could no longer restrain himself.

"Amber, you may hate me for saying this, but I despise Sam Reynolds for what he has done to you!"

Amber was too flabbergasted to answer, but her heart took a great bound upward! He did still care, at least a little. Taking both hands, she gathered her courage together and spoke in a very small voice.

"I don't love Sam Reynolds in any way except as a good friend and as Crystal's husband-to-be."

Robert shot a glance at her then concentrated on his driving. "Oh?"

He certainly wasn't going to make it any easier for her, Amber thought. His wall of reserve was a mountain between them. It was up to her to penetrate that wall. Their future happiness depended on it.

She desperately closed both eyes tight and plunged in.

"The ring . . . that day . . . I thought you meant Crystal."

"Crystal?" His response was as cool as the night air slipping in through the partly open window.

"Don't be so icy!" Amber's control was gone. "I saw you in LaGrande. I thought you loved her and had bought the ring for

217

her. How could I think otherwise? Crystal told me the whole story today."

With great care Robert pulled the car into the front yard at the Crossroads Clinic. There was nothing icy about him as he reached for her. As long as she lived Amber would remember the look in his eyes just before he kissed her, gently at first, then with deep feeling, until she felt she would burst with happiness. The feel of something cool slipping onto her ring finger caused her to look down. There was the ring he had bought so long ago.

"You carried it? In spite of . . ."

"Yes," Robert teased, devilment in his eyes. "First to remind me how foolish I had been to ever hope for your love. Or am I still?"

"Forever, Robert." It was enough. Robert whirled the car like a madman, heading back down the road toward the Lostine cutoff to the Carter ranch.

"Where are we going?" Amber managed to gasp.

"We're going back to the Carters," Robert replied grimly, but with a twinkle in his eye. "We're going to get them out of bed and tell them it's going to be a double wedding Saturday night. I'm not taking any more chances with you!"

Amber asked meekly, "And just how do you propose to get a license? And a dress for me? And all those necessities every bride needs?"

With mock severity he glared at her.

"I'll tend to the license, the preacher, and the honeymoon. You can take care of the rest." He scowled ferociously.

"Woman, I won't rest until you're my meek, obedient, humble bride."

Amber couldn't help but laugh at his foolishness. It was wonderful just to laugh again! But all the wind went out of his sails when she whispered, "Yes, Robert. I love you."

CHAPTER 16

After the first gasp of surprise the Carters congratulated Robert and Amber heartily.

"About time," Billy said, freckles standing out more than ever. Charlie, in the background with Bruno, only smiled. He had just turned fifteen, and was learning not to blurt out everything he thought.

Crystal didn't speak, only looked at Amber with eyes full of understanding. Sam was glad — he had no way of knowing all the couple had gone through on his account!

And so it was arranged. The Saturday wedding would be double. Amber and Crystal went into a huddle, coming up with Mrs. Carter's wedding dress for Amber, if she cared to wear it. She did.

"It's lovely," she told Mrs. Carter, fingering the delicate lace. She couldn't have pleased Mrs. Carter more with a million dollars. On the way home Amber's joy couldn't be contained.

"If I had only known happiness was just around the corner this would have been a far different spring," she told Robert. It seemed as though a cloud now drifted back over her unhappiness, gently shrouding the lonely days and nights both she and Robert had spent apart.

Before she felt quite ready, Saturday was there. Only a valley inhabitant could know the beauty of May 1, Amber thought as she rose early. She was too happy to sleep. Her wedding day! She breathed a quick prayer, "May Robert and I always work together and make our lives count in the total plan of things with the skills you have given us."

Her heart sang praises and as she finished the last little things to be done before leaving her clinic home, she stopped to look out the window at the clear sunshine and fleecy blossoms. In spite of her joy there was a sharp little pain at the thought of her leaving. This had been home for so long. In it were all the joys and sorrows of girlhood. Now she was leaving. Never again would Amber sleep in the pleasant room that had been hers. Never again would she curl up on the couch in front of the fireplace. A mist rose in her eyes, but as Robert's face swam to her consciousness, Amber smiled tremulously. She was going to a new life, but the old would be with her. The beloved books, Tawny, her father's picture . . . a hundred other memories and little invisible chains would ease the transition from girl to woman, from maiden to wife.

The ring of the telephone shattered her reflections. It was Robert, his voice worried.

"Amber, I don't know what to say. There's been an accident. My housekeeper fell down the stairs and is hurt badly. Most of the doctors have gone to Portland for a medical convention, Dr. Mitchell included. She needs us, Amber, but it's our wedding day!"

For a moment Amber was still, but only for a moment.

"I'll be right there," she promised. Quickly she donned her uniform, turning from the sight of her wedding dress waiting in the closet. What did it matter if their wedding was postponed? A human life was in need, and a beloved one at that.

Amber would never know that although Robert had loved her before, more than he thought possible, yet that day her instant decision added an element of worship to his feelings. While the other couple were exchanging vows Robert and Amber were battling for life. The housekeeper had evidently lain at the foot of the stairs for some time, blood pouring from her head. She was very weak, her pulse was thready, her breathing shallow.

It was touch and go, but after Robert had finished repairing the damaged head he turned to Amber with hope in his face.

"I think she'll make it." Amber heaved a sigh of relief. Her adept fingers had handed necessary instruments to Robert, watching with usual anticipation his swift movements, anticipating his needs until he didn't have to ask. This is where I belong, she thought happily. By Robert's side. Doing the work I've been given to do, using the training I have, helping him, working together, for others. The memory of the wedding faded from her vision. Again she and Robert had stood at a crossroads. Would life be full of them? she wondered. Was it a series of deciding whether left or right, stop or go? Perhaps it was. If so, she prayed they would always choose the right way for them.

During the long hours waiting for the outcome of surgery, Robert and Amber sat quietly, each lost in thought. Robert had been disappointed, understandably so, by the wedding's postponement. Yet as he looked at the still, white figure on the bed he couldn't regret their decision. She had done a lot for him; if he could repay with his talents, it was worth it all.

Amber reflected on the wedding that had taken place without them. She expected Sam and Crystal to have a good life. Both had learned the importance of giving, not only of time and talent, but of themselves. What a winter and spring it had been! How much they had all learned! She had learned the true meaning of her father's motto only when faced with the necessity of sharing it. Deep inside she wondered why she was so blessed. I'm just an ordinary person, one small piece of humanity, yet I feel the whole world is mine. It's because of Robert, she thought. He has changed drab to delight, winter to spring in my heart. She smiled at him tenderly. He had turned to look out the window and was silhouetted against the brilliant picture formed outside by spring dressing. A slight moan recalled them both to duty.

"It's all right," Robert assured the woman on the bed, who had opened her eyes. "Just rest." There was comfort in his voice, and with a small sigh she closed her eyes and slept, this time a natural sleep. They were free to go off duty.

Early evening had fallen as they drove back to the Crossroads Clinic on what would have been their wedding day. Purple shadows outlined the mountains in the distance, a rosy light provided background for the trees in bloom. Amber leaned her head against Robert's shoulder contentedly. It had been a good day. She could honestly say there was no disappointment in her. Tentatively they made plans. Both wanted to stay as long as they were needed; then, too, Sam and Crystal would never forgive them if they were married while the other couple were honeymooning!

"Would you want to wait two weeks?" the girl asked, anxiously peering into the beloved face above her, again noting the lines of tiredness around his eyes and mouth.

"I would wait forever." The answer was simple and direct. In it was all the longing of years of loving her, often hopelessly, with pain, and uncertainty. Quick tears sprang to her eyes.

"Poor Robert! Why didn't I know sooner there could never have been anyone else but you? Why did it take me so long to realize that the dreams I held were all centered around someone 'just like Robert'? Why did I have to hurt you, and be mean, and jealous? Why, Robert, why?"

He thought for a long time, then spoke softly. "Amber, if we had married before part of the work you were meant to do might have remained unfinished. In time we will want children, and I know you will want to be with them as much as you can. Your nursing will be part-time, or on call for their growing-up years. You're too much of a homemaker for it to be otherwise. Yet you will keep on with your nursing, too. I can't see you being unwilling to share your skill. Especially in the outlying districts. Those people love, trust, and need you.

"Suppose you had been married and busy with children when Charlie Vickers needed you. Or Sally May with her little Amber Lee. Or even Vagabond Vic. Don't you see? You were needed more there at that time even than I needed you. It's all part of a plan. But now it's time for us. We can work together as husband and wife should, sharing, caring. We can have the same kind of marriage your father and mother had until she died. Gradually the 'me' will become 'we' and together our lives can count."

Amber was too choked up to tell him this was exactly what she had been thinking those long hours at the hospital. Later there would be time. Years would come and go and still they would be together, as he had said, caring . . . sharing . . . giving.

When the first excitement had settled down, Amber was glad of the two weeks' grace before her wedding. Now she had time to finish some of the things a normal bride gets done! She stayed in her little clinic cottage, giving it a thorough cleaning for the next occupant. She had no idea who it would be. Then one evening at dusk Robert and Dr. Mitchell came over.

"Amber, if you're agreeable we know what to do about your living quarters." There was suppressed excitement about both of them.

Amber lifted an eyebrow. "Yes?"

Dr. Mitchell spoke heartily. "Amber, my niece from Boise has just finished her training. She's tired from the long years of study and doesn't want to go right into full-time city hospital nursing. Also, her mother, my sister, needs to be away from some of the hustle and bustle for a while. She's getting old and tired. If you agree, I'd like to bring them here. It's just the right size for them, and" — a gleam shot through his eyes — "if Lynn can keep away from nursing once she's here, I'll eat my hat! I know you're first love is back-country nursing and what with marriage to this oaf" — he poked Robert — "you'll have enough to do. I thought I could ask Lynn to work in the office here."

"That's splendid," Amber cried, eyes sparkling. "I've wondered and wondered how I could keep up both ends of my bargain!" She cast a demure glance at her fiancé. "While Robert is marrying a nurse, I think he probably also hopes he's marrying a woman, not a machine. This would give me some time for him." A lovely blush mantled her face and was echoed in Robert's.

By the time Amber's wedding day came, this time unmarred by sickness or trouble, Lynn and her mother were eagerly packing.

Amber had fallen in love with Lynn at first sight when the girl had come for a get-acquainted visit. The twinkle in her blue eyes matched Amber's own, her raven hair fell to her firm shoulders, held back by a simple clasp while she was on duty. In turn, Lynn admired Amber immensely. She could see the work that was being done. It didn't take long for her to realize that if she was seeking challenges, this was the country for them! Then, too, the reaction of the male population, which had suffered a blight with Crystal and Amber being removed from circulation, certainly was reassuring. It was surprising how many people, many of them young men, found it urgent to consult Miss Amber on one thing or another when Lynn was there. Amber complained laughingly she couldn't go out the door without falling over them!

Sam and Crystal arrived back the day

before the wedding, radiant, unbelievably happy. It had been beautiful at the Coast. To Crystal, who had spent most of her life in the valley, the vast expanse of Pacific Ocean was a never-ending source of joy.

"But I'd have been equally happy if Sam had wanted to go to the mountains, or desert, or lion hunting!" she admitted to Amber.

Amber smiled at her effervescence, then reminded, "Crystal, you did something for me even greater than telling me about Robert just before you were married. Do you remember what it was?"

A perplexed look touched Crystal's happy features lightly. "No, Amber. What?"

Amber's eyes were sober. "You told me it wouldn't matter where or how you lived if you really loved someone, that it would be enough just being with him. It took me a long time to accept it, but deep inside I knew you were right. Then when I was all alone in that dreadful cabin with Vic and Satan I thought about it squarely. If that wasn't the way a person cared, then they really didn't care much." She swallowed a sob.

"When Satan attacked Robert I knew that without him life wouldn't be worth living."

Crystal patted her hand. "Don't cry,

Amber. It's all over now. Look!" She pointed out the open window to where a rainbow arched the heavens. "Rainbow after rain. It's always that way. It takes the showers to clear the air so the rainbow can come, promising sunshine."

Again Amber was struck by the great change in Crystal. Warmly she told her, "I'm glad we've become friends."

Crystal nodded, blonde curls dancing. "Me, too!"

Again the hours rushed by and then it was another glorious morning. Everything was in readiness. Amber would dress in her wedding gown at the clinic cottage, the last time for her there. Afterward she would go to Robert's, no, their home, she corrected herself, and change to go away.

No one knew their honeymoon plans, just that they were going far enough away so they couldn't be reached by telephone! Robert had asked Amber her preference and she had rather sheepishly told him, "It doesn't matter. Whatever you want." Finally they agreed their plans would just be not to make plans! After the initial drive down the beautiful Columbia River to Portland, their destination would be wherever they felt like it. They were just going to wander for about two or three weeks. Maybe the Coast for a few days, maybe even into the edge of Canada.

"You know what this is," Amber accused, grinning broadly. "It's a revolt against the schedules we keep! Against the rushing from one place to another in the line of duty, the pressure, the keeping on keeping on!"

Robert agreed, then kissed her once more.

Amber thought of their conversation as she dressed. It was early, but she had a visit to make. When she was arrayed in the beautiful gown she quietly slipped out the door the last time, hesitating on the threshold of her new life.

"Good-bye, little girl Amber. Maybe someday I will have one like you." Laughing at her own nonsense, she stepped into Robert's car. No jeep for her today! Carefully settling her gown around her, she drove away. One more errand, then her wedding!

CHAPTER 17

The lone figure etched against the early-summer sky caught her cobwebby draperies closer against a gentle breeze. Trembling with happiness, she knelt beside the small stone in the simple country graveyard. The inscription was engraved on her heart as well as the headstone:

DAVID MACKENZIE
who accepted the
Crossroads Calling

How little the words told of the man who had lived and loved, had suffered and known joy!

Amber had taken the precaution of bringing an old blanket with her. Now she gently traced the carving with her forefinger, looking around. She wanted to remember every detail of this final girlhood meeting with her father. After today Robert would come with her, and in time, perhaps a small David, Robert, or Amber. But now belonged to her alone. Even Robert must wait. She had felt a compulsion about coming here in her wedding gown. When she walked down the aisle of the little church it would be on Don Baker's arm. He had been pleased when she asked him. But these few moments were not for looking ahead, but back. She remembered a class motto one of the graduating classes had chosen: "Look to the future, but remember the past."

How fitting! And yet, without the past there could be no future. It didn't seem strange to speak aloud. No one was near. She was glad for that. It would never do for "young Mrs. Dr. Robert," as she would be known, to be seen kneeling by a grave in her wedding gown. Scandalous!

"I don't care," she told the passing breeze, lifting her face proudly to the cloudless sky and letting the peace of the quiet earth sink into her very being.

"It is proper," she reassured a songbird who had stopped to fill the world with a caroling melody. He ignored her and went on singing.

Amber smiled, then surveyed the countryside almost as if she had never seen it before. Rolling hills, giving way to deeper green mountains, then snowcapped distant peaks. Quite different from the scene Sam had described when he first came to the valley so long ago.

How much had happened! The evening before Crystal had confided that a leading publishing company was very interested in Sam's *Two Ways for the Traveler.*

"Even though it's fiction, you won't fail to recognize your father as the pattern Sam used for the hero," she added quietly, eyes misting. "Amber, I can never tell you what it means to me to see that book written. It is a triumph of good over evil. In today's world when so much sordid and sick hits the market, it is inspirational to find an editor who wants to examine and who will express interest in such a story."

Amber felt again the warmth of Crystal's story. She marveled at the influence her father had had on people, and continued to have! If Sam could capture in a book, and somehow she believed he had done just that, the feelings her father had come to have, the world would be a little better place because of it.

"Dad, it's my turn now. I can't lean on your ideas. I have to express my own. It's up to me to live the way you taught me, to be honest and caring. And yet, you taught

234

Robert, too. It won't even be hard." She was still for a moment, her thoughts far away from the peaceful scene before her.

"Even if I knew there was nothing more, I would still live my life exactly as you taught, in service of others. The only real happy people are those who give. I remember what Sam said in one of our early conversations. 'You are the happiest person I know . . . because you have hope. I'd give anything I possess to have that.' Dad, now he does. He has learned the power of the words written on your stone. I don't know much about where you are, even though I believe within me that you exist. I don't know if you can hear me. It doesn't really matter. All that matters is that your teachings will live on in me, and in my children, and in their children. You've given us a heritage that will be passed on from generation to generation."

Amber fell silent, too deeply touched even for words. Although she had come to in a sense say good-bye to part of her life, in talking aloud she realized there was nothing to say good-bye to! It was all still part of her, and always would be. It wasn't until a faint chime in the distance reminded her of the time of day that she stood and looked down at the grassy plot, and quoted the words she had chosen to live by:

"A traveler came to a crossroads. Two
    ways met.
One led to fame and fortune . . . and yet
He paused, unable to choose.

The right way, or the left?
What had he to lose?

At last he decided which way his feet
    would trod,
He chose the right way, to happiness . . .
    and God."

Tears blinded her, but they were tears of
happiness, appreciation for all she had been
given. With a prayer for worthiness she
turned. A few paces away stood Robert. He
had come for her. A great gladness filled
her heart as he came to her side, and
together they started down the path that
would lead into the future. But at the bottom they paused and looked back to where
the songbird's mate had now joined him,
raising her voice with his in praise to the
summer sky.

We hope you have enjoyed this Large Print book. Other Thorndike, Wheeler, and Chivers Press Large Print books are available at your library or directly from the publishers.

For information about current and upcoming titles, please call or write, without obligation, to:

Publisher
Thorndike Press
295 Kennedy Memorial Drive
Waterville, ME 04901
Tel. (800) 223-1244

or visit our Web site at:

http://gale.cengage.com/thorndike

OR

Chivers Large Print
published by BBC Audiobooks Ltd
St James House, The Square
Lower Bristol Road
Bath BA2 3SB
England
Tel. +44(0) 800 136919
email: bbcaudiobooks@bbc.co.uk
www.bbcaudiobooks.co.uk

All our Large Print titles are designed for easy reading, and all our books are made to last.